The Water War

© Marc Alexander

ISBN 978-1-909473-12-6

Text prepared by www.willowebooks.org.uk

The Water War

by

Marc Alexander

Published by Willow Books

For my fine old pals
Harry Darton and Dick Sharples

CHAPTER 1

Luke Muldoon, poised between sky and earth on the rim of the valley, looked down grimly on the herd of cattle grazing below. The merciless sun made the sweat trickle down his neck as he edged his rifle into position. With the habit of an old buffalo hunter he licked his finger and wet the foresight of the Sharps. Then he selected a heavy looking steer and squinted down the barrel at it with a skilled marksman's surety.

Muldoon's finger tightened. The crash of the Sharps echoed and re-echoed in the valley. The steer reared and toppled. The gunshot caused the cattle to toss their heads in surprise. A few on the edge of the herd began to run aimlessly. Muldoon fired again and a long-horned cow began to stagger in small circles until she sank to the ground.

Again and again the lone sniper fired into the milling cattle and, as the number of carcases grew, a thin smile creased his leathery face.

A pall of dust now hung over the bewildered cattle and Muldoon waited some moments for it to settle before firing his final shot. Then, with his sights on a large black steer, he fired and laughed aloud over the long barrel of the buffalo gun as he saw the beast sink to its knees.

Luke Muldoon wriggled back from the valley edge and climbed to his feet when he knew he would not make a silhouette against the cloudless, shimmering sky. But as he turned the smile of savage satisfaction froze on his face. Before him were two cowpunchers, each with a Colt pointing directly at his belly.

"Waal, if it ain't Mister Muldoon," began one conversationally. "Them animals you been droppin' ain't buffaloes, Muldoon."

"Speakin' personal, I'd put him as a rustler," said the second. "One way or another he's done the boss out of a dozen beeves."

"I ain't been rustlin' no beeves. I bin shootin' 'em, as I said I would. For every beeve of mine that died of thirst I swore to God I'd shoot a Circle-Star beast. Today I found a dozen of my steers dead so I've done just that. I've picked off a dozen in the valley, an' unless Boss Quinn lets water through there'll be a goddam sight more."

The two punchers regarded him for nearly a minute in silence, their guns unwavering. Then one said: "Seems to me shootin' the steers is as bad as rustlin' 'em."

"You know what happens to rustlers," drawled the other, touching his coiled lariat with his left hand.

"I ain't been a-rustling and you varmints know it," yelled Muldoon. "My quarrel ain't with you, it's with your boss."

"Gimme your gun," snapped the first, ignoring this line of reasoning.

Muldoon passed up the Sharps butt first. He had not had time to reload it so it was useless to him anyway.

"Got any other ironmongery?"

"Ain't had any use for a handgun," retorted Muldoon scornfully. "I'm an old hunter, not a man-killer. Now, boys, I reckon I got a right to a fair trial. You take me to the marshal and I'll cause you no trouble. The trial will bring the whole durned problem into the open,"

"Okay, Muldoon," said the first Circle-Star rider. "We won't string you up right now. We won't take you to the marshal either. You come and see Boss Quinn first."

"I want a trial fair and square," replied the old rifleman. "I won't stand a cat's chance in hell with Boss Quinn."

"You shoulda thought of that when you got his

cattle in your sights. Now get going down that trail."

Muttering to himself, the prisoner began to walk along a path that led from the edge of the valley. It twisted between some clumps of gnarled trees and as Muldoon approached them he decided to act, knowing that the branches would hinder the horses. He sprinted to the right but before he could gain shelter two Colts exploded as one. A .45 Peacemaker slug smashed his spine. His body jerked grotesquely and he plunged forward, the first casualty in the Water War.

* * *

Boss Quinn sat on the veranda of his sprawling house. It was not the sort of place that one would expect the owner of over a hundred square miles of rangeland to have. It was crude and ugly, and despite its size, there was something about it that put the onlooker in mind of a log cabin. Beyond the veranda could be seen the yellow lights of the long, low bunkhouse and cookhouse, and further on still were the vague shapes of the other ranch buildings merging into the deep purple of the hot night.

The man who owned the Circle-Star was short and bulky. His head, with its mane of silver hair and spade-shaped beard, seemed heavy even for his broad shoulders. The eyes were glittering points of cold blue and there was about him an atmosphere of restless power. Before him sat a younger man. He was tall and graceful in his bearing, with clean-cut features that were a direct contrast to Boss Quinn's craggy face. One thing the two men had in common was the sheen of sweat on their skins, for the nights of the great drought of 1883 were hot and prickly.

"So, Reverend, what has made you come the long journey from your holding to see me?" said the master of the Circle-Star, carefully inspecting the glowing tip of his long cigar.

"Please drop that title," said the young man. "It is

3

true that on the Lord's Day I sometimes preach the Word. But I have not been ordained a minister of God – yet."

"Okay, Mister Royle, if that suits you better," rumbled Boss Quinn. "Out with it."

"I've come because of what happened yesterday. Because two of your men murdered Luke Muldoon."

"The word 'murder' is a mighty strong one, Rev. – er – Mister Royle. It makes me figure you've come out here about something you don't rightly savvy."

"You're right. Mister Quinn," responded Ethan Royle. "I sure don't understand why one of the Lord's creatures was cruelly done to death, an' I don't understand why you are ruinin' the ranches here."

"Now we're coming to it," said Boss Quinn. "You don't understand why I built my dam."

"That, too. Water belongs to God. No man can own what is God's."

"You're pretty new here, Mister Royle," rumbled Quinn, dragging on his cigar so his face was briefly lit by a strange red glow. "Most of the little ranchers are pretty new here."

"Now you've mebbe heard a lot about me when you ride on your buckboard into Silver Bend. You've most likely heard a lot of complaints from the smallholders. But right now, son, I'm gonna tell you the story from my side. Then maybe you won't be quite so ready to holler murder. But first of all, one thing I want you to get your loop around pronto. Luke Muldoon was a durned fool who got what he was lookin' for. He shot twelve of my beeves when my boys found him. Some ranchers'd claim they was in their rights if they'd strung him up then and there, but my men were gonna bring him in and let him stand fair trial. It was only when he bolted they fired."

"But why was he shootin' your cattle?" demanded Royle. "Because he was a desperate man. Because he had

4

been driven beyond the limits of human endurance as he watched his cattle die. He had one of the outlyin' holdings, so his creek was the first to dry out after you built your dam. You drove him to do what he did."

"Mister Royle, I did no such thing. Just you listen to me for a few minutes and then judge."

Boss Quinn settled his powerful bulk back in his chair and looked up to the stars which were now glittering above as if he searching for inspiration.

"When I was a kid, around ten years, my parents came West in an old covered wagon," he said. "I remember my Ma sittin' up in the front, my baby sister in her lap, the reins in her hands, while my Dad drove his little herd of fifty head. That was forty-five years ago.

"This land was wild, the home of the buffalo and the redskin. There weren't no settlers in this district at all in them days. My Dad was the first to come here. He brought a lot of trade goods so he could make friends with the Indians. At first they let him stay with his tiny herd. He built his cabin right here where we're sitting now. Mebbe the Indians thought he would soon starve and quit. They didn't bother him much. They just took all they could in trade goods and at night they might drive off a steer or two when they felt like it. Made a change from buffalo meat.

"Well, it didn't take long for the herd to be reduced to half and I remember every night my father would round up the cattle into a corral and keep watch over them with a rifle, while my mother – trying not to show me how scared she was – bolted the door and kept a pistol within reach.

"One night a party of braves tried to drive off a steer when Dad saw them. He upped with his rifle and shot one. A few days later we was raided. I can see it as if it was happening now. My Dad was away from the house and I remember this band of redskins whooping down the

5

valley an' surroundin' the house. My Ma slammed the door and began firing through the window. The braves fired back with arrows, some of them blazing in an attempt to set the house on fire.

"I remember my Ma kissin' me, pushing me out of a little window at the back. 'You hide in the rain barrel, Bill,' she said. I was pretty scared but I did what she said. I climbed in the half-filled butt and pulled the lid over my head. The firing and the shouting went on for a long time. And then there was a silence and then some screamin'. I never saw Ma again, or Jenny.

"All day long I shivered in that damn butt and finally I could not stop myself from cryin' any longer. I began to howl like a coyote. Suddenly the lid was lifted off and I expected to see a face covered with warpaint, a hand holdin' a tomahawk to bash my head in. But it was Dad. Behind him the stars were shinin' just like they are now. 'Don't cry, Billy,' he said, but I could see there were tears streamin' down his face. 'I'm gonna take you away from all this and some day, son, we're gonna come back here an' reclaim our land.'

"Well, he lifted me out an' held me by the hand. Most of the cabin was a charred ruin and the horses were gone. So we walked for several days, movin' mainly by night because Dad was scared a war party'd be out lookin' for him. I can't remember all that journey. God knows how we lived. Dad carried me a lot of the way in his arms. He was some man, because I must have been twelve years old by then.

"We finally made it back to an outpost and I figure Dad must have got some sort of roustabout job to keep us. He saved up enough to get the gear to go prospectin'. He went off for some time and he struck pay dirt. It wasn't a bonanza, but it was enough for what he wanted. He bought another small herd and hired some men and armed them to the teeth. He brought his men and wagons back to

6

this valley and built this house.

"You can see it ain't very pretty because it was built as a fort. See them iron shutters with the loopholes in? Any sign of trouble and they'd be bolted into place over the windows. With enough ammunition for a small war, and durned great casks of water and food he could have held out against the whole Indian nation for months. The braves did attack but Dad and his men – what a hard bunch of *hombres* they were – managed to beat them off.

"When the raid was over Dad decided to teach 'em a lesson. He led a raid on an Indian village and burned it. I remember him ridin' back and I suddenly realised what sort of man he was – he was iron inside and out. He tousled my hair with a hand covered with Indian blood. His clothing stank of smoke. He said: 'You won't have to hide in any more butts, Billy. An' I've evened the score for Ma and Jenny.'

"The redskins didn't bother us too much after that. Maybe they'd kill a rangerider or try an' rustle some of our beeves, but they never attacked this place again. I guess they'd learned to respect Pa, seein' he could beat them at their own game of massacre. We raised our cattle and built up a pretty big herd. There was no one else on the range in them days, and we took all the land we needed.

"Then one day when I was about twenty, Dad's horse came galloping into the corral with an empty saddle. Me and the boys rode off in the direction he'd come and about a mile from the ranchhouse we found him. He'd been ambushed and shot through with an arrow, but he'd got clear before the loss of blood had weakened him and he'd fallen from the saddle. He was dyin' as I bent over him. 'It's my turn to go, son,' he said, 'You see that the Quinns keep this range. It's been paid for with my blood and the blood of your Ma.'

"I didn't have time to promise him 'cause he just

7

closed his eyes and died. But right there and then I knew that nothing on this earth would take the Circle-Star away from me."

He paused and lit another cigar.

"But, Mister Quinn," said Ethan Royle, "if you saw so much misfortune yourself, you should be tolerant of others when trouble comes their way."

"Yep, and I guess you'd like me to turn the other cheek, when some varmint starts shooting down my cows," he snorted. "Well, listen a mite longer. To understand my dam you've got to understand the territory the Circle-Star covers. After Dad died I took over and worked like a durn slave to build up the ranch. There were setbacks. Once we lost over a thousand head in a blizzard. Another season it was cattle fever. Next a gang of rustlers got to work until we strung them up on that corral gate over there. One way or another it was always a battle. And yet we built up the Circle-Star so that it covered most of The Plateau. And remember there wasn't hardly any other settlers. The land was free to be taken. It was just a question of holding it. And by God we sure held it. And now, if you look at the map, son, you'll see that The Plateau is cut by a series of valleys down which runs the Snowy River. It starts at Mount Snowy to the north and it's fed from the snow cap. Cuts through my land, through my valleys and it comes out of The Plateau country a couple of miles south of here where it splits into a network of creeks that wander off across the plains."

"I know that," said Ethan Royle a little impatiently. "One of those creeks feeds my holding and it's been dryin' up through the summer. We're almost into autumn and there ain't been any rain, an' unless it rains soon those creeks'll be pathways of dry mud, thanks to your dam."

"Yep," mused Boss Quinn. "Like the others, you are blamin' me for the drought. Listen a bit more then. I had to depend on the Snowy River for my water and when

8

I say my water I mean just that. Old Snowy is part of the Circle-Star territory so it's Circle-Star water. When the drought came the level soon dropped. The volume was less than half what it was. So there was only one thing for me to do. I did exactly what my Pa did when he built this house. I prepared for siege. I threw a dam across the Snowy to build a reservoir.

"Damn it, I'd every right to. It's my land and my water. Why the hell should I lose my stock because a lot of Johnnies-come-lately object? It ain't as though I cut off the water completely. There's still water going over the sluices. It's just that I've built up a lake so that I can bring my stock down and water them. It wouldn't make any difference to the smallholders if the dam wasn't there. The creeks would be dryin' up just the same. I know. We had a drought here twenty years back and we saved ourselves with a dam then. But then there weren't any little ranchers. The range hadn't been tamed for them. It was only after the Circle-Star made this territory safe that they dared, to come here and build their homes and string up their blamed barbed wire."

Ethan Royle shifted uncomfortably in his chair. He'd been impressed by Boss Quinn's story and yet as a smallholder himself he knew the anguish of watching his creek level drop daily until his cows had to wade out through stinking mud to drink at the brackish trickle. Already the cattle were dying on the outlying holdings and men like Luke Muldoon faced ruin. It was not worth shipping the cattle off. The price had fallen from thirty dollars a head, last season's price, to eight dollars and less.

There was a glut on the market due to the drought. If the small rancher was to stay in business he had to some-how keep his cattle alive until the next season. And it made Ethan Royle, man of peace that he was, full of wrath to think of his own scrawny beasts compared with the prime cattle of the Circle-Star who were watered at the artificial lake.

"If that dam wasn't there, there'd be more water in the creeks," he said stubbornly. "You must remember that water doesn't belong to one man. Water belongs to God and all are equal in His eyes."

Boss Quinn laughed grimly, his features like some Old Testament patriarch in his cigar glow. "Firstly, if that dam went the creeks might fill up for half a day – no more. Secondly, I seem to recollect from readin' the Bible that when the children of Israel was in the desert the Lord took a mighty individual interest in their welfare. When they was fightin' the Caananites, He sure didn't regard all men as equal."

The young man said nothing for a while. He was trying to think of an argument that would halt the trouble he knew must come. From out of the doorway of the house a young woman stepped, carrying a tray. On it was a whisky bottle and a jug of coffee.

"Good evening, Mister Royle," came a soft, husky voice. "I've brought Dad his nightcap but I knew you would prefer coffee."

"Thank you, Miss Quinn," said Ethan Royle, rising. "I guess you must have heard that I do not take strong drink."

"I certainly had, Mister Royle," she smiled. "I once heard you preach in Silver Bend."

There was not enough light to see her features clearly but Royle knew them to be classically perfect. As perfect as her gowned figure appeared silhouetted in the open doorway of light. Her black hair gleamed in a wave that swept down to her shoulders and in the hot drought air her cool perfume was a faint relief. Royle knew that Ella Quinn was one of the most admired young women in the territory and considered by many connoisseurs of feminine charms to be as much a beauty as his own fair-

10

haired wife. But it would have been a mighty brave suitor who would try and take her hand under the jealous eye of her father who loved his only child with the same passion as he loved his great ranch.

"Is this young man a good preacher then?" asked Boss Quinn. "I'll admit he had some guts coming out here and accusin' my boys of murder."

"He was too good," laughed Ella. "I dreamt about hell fire for days after."

"I guess Silver Bend could use a bit of Bible-thumpin'," growled the boss of the Circle-Star. "If the smallholders spent more time at their ranches instead of drinkin' Red Eye in the Good Luck Saloon they'd be makin' out better than they're doin'."

"I guess despair makes men take to vicious ways," muttered Royle. "It drives them to violence and that's what I'm afraid of, Mister Quinn. I'm afraid things will reach a pitch that it'll be too late to do anything. The men will take the law into their own hands."

"You're sayin' there will be a war over my dam?" queried Quinn.

"I'm sayin' just that. Smallholders are forming the Silver Bend Cattlemen's Protection Association. And there's men involved in that who would welcome violence."

"Well, I've faced Indians, disease, drought and rustlers. So I ain't exactly scared when you tell me about Silver Bend Cattlemen's Protection Association," said Boss Quinn, in sardonic humour at the thought. "Tell me, son, why are you so concerned? There's still some water in your creek and you don't seem to me to be the usual whinin' smallholder. Where do you fit in this?"

"I don't want to see trouble.," said Ethan Royle. "Out here in the West the Colt has been king too long. Gun law must go. We must start gettin' law and justice and civilisation. There must be a new era here for our kids

11

to grow up in. You ask me where I fit in. Well, I guess I hate violence."

In the dim light Boss Quinn looked hard at his open face. "What do you know about violence?" he asked. "I bet you ain't never toted a gun in your life."

"Maybe I ain't, Mister Quinn, but there's someone in my family who has and I've seen enough unhappiness through it. The wages of sin is death, Mister Quinn. Now, what can I tell the boys in Silver Bend?"

"You can tell 'em that anyone who shoots my beeves will end up doin' a jig at the end of a lariat. You can tell 'em that on my land I'll do what I durned well like. Like you, Mister Royle, I don't like trouble, but I'm used to it. I aim to keep my stock watered even if they send the U.S. Cavalry against me."

Ethan Royle stood up. "I guess my visit has been a waste .of time.," he said. "You can't see beyond the Circle-Star territory."

"And what's wrong with that?"

Royle shrugged sadly. "There's gonna be trouble and everyone's goin' to think they're in the right."

"Isn't that always the case, Mister Royle?" said Ella from the shadows.

" Goodnight," said the young man, turning to walk down the steps.

"Mister Royle," came the voice of Boss Quinn. "I have one word of advice."

"Yes?"

"Dig a well."

CHAPTER 2

Bluish smoke from the small fire rose in a pencil line in the hot air. On the glowing embers rested a frying pan in which beans and bacon gave forth a mouth-watering smell. Lounging against a rock in the shade a man dressed in range-riding clothes picked up the empty bean can.

He was tall and loose-knit, and his fair, sun bleached hair fell across his forehead. Though still young, his features were lined round the eyes and there were clefts each side of his mouth. It gave him a strange, worn appearance and his blue eyes, though piercing, had a faded look. For a moment he regarded the can, then with his left hand sent it spinning skywards.

As it reached the apex of its flight, a gun in the stranger's right hand exploded. The bullet punched the can and sent it higher and, as it began to fall back to earth, the gun crashed again, sending it soaring. Again and again the Colt .44 barked and each time the twisted tin described a glittering arc in the sky. As the last bullet whined into the coppery heavens and the perforated metal plummeted down for the final time, a second gun crashed in the background and the can spun crazily sideways and clattered among the rocks.

The first marksman, uncomfortably aware that his gun was now empty, looked over his shoulder to see a slim, dark-bearded man sitting on a bay horse, a smoking gun dangling at the end of a limp arm.

"Howdy," he said. "Excuse me for getting in on the act, but when I saw you perforating that airtight I couldn't resist. My name's Sam Cash."

The first man regarded him a moment with bleak eyes. Then he said: "Howdy. The name's Royle. Lee

13

Royle. That was a pretty nice shot. There ain't many guys could have done that. Could you use some beans?"

"I sure could at that," said Cash, bolstering his gun in a beautifully tooled Mexican holster. He swung gracefully down from the saddle. "That's mighty neighbourly of you, *compadre*," he continued. "I've got a bottle of Old Vermont that should help it down."

He walked stiff legged over to Royle. The two men clasped hands for the briefest moment, then Cash sprawled down in the shade of a rock, his eyes squinting in the glare of the midday sun.

"Come far?" asked Royle in a voice that showed politeness rather than curiosity.

"Aha, I'm heading for Silver Bend. I got a job waitin' for roe with the Circle-Star. Say, that was some nice gun-work you was doing. With ammunition the price it is, you must enjoy lettin' it off."

Royle lazily stirred the beans. "I've been without a gun for a while and now I've got this new one."

Sam Cash said nothing. There would only be one reason why such a marksman would be without a gun. Royle squinted at the pistol in his hand.

"Way back, I used to have an old .45 Dragoon," he said. "I could do anything with that gun. Now I got this new Frontier but somehow I ain't quite got the balance of it yet."

"Could've fooled me, the way you kept that can going up and down," laughed Sam Cash. "As you see, I use a Navy Colt myself. But most fellas seem to like the Frontier."

"It feels just like the Peacemaker," said Royle. "Except being a .44 instead of a .45 you can use Winchester ammunition in it, I guess it's an advantage not havin' to tote round two lots of cartridges. Anyway, these beans look as if they're ready. Got a plate?"

Sam Cash took a tin plate and a bottle out of his

saddle-bag. For a while the men sat cross-legged, too busy eating to waste breath on conversation. When the meal was finished and the tin plates were like mirrors, Sam Cash passed his bottle over to Royle.

"You know, the finest bit of shootin' I've ever seen in my life was with a .41 double-action Colt," he said, "and the guy who was using it was William Bonney."

"You knew Billy the Kid then?" asked Royle.

"*Si*. I've swapped lead with him over Lincoln County way. But I never had no hard feelin's agin 'im. You were either on one side or the other in the Lincoln County War. An' I got my pay from the other side, that's all.

"I was in Lincoln when Billy bust out of jail," continued Cash, taking his turn at the bottle. "Yeah, no matter how long I live, I'll never see anythin' like that again. They were keepin' Billy upstairs of the old courthouse, and they weren't takin' no chances 'cause he had heavy leg irons on. One of the guards, Bob Ollinger, was an old enemy of Billy's and he sure made the best of the situation. He knew that Billy would be due for the gallows in a few days and he did everything he could to remind him of it. He even used to sit there tyin' hangman's nooses in front of him.

"Well, this particular day Ollinger went across the road to the hotel opposite to have his lunch, an' Billy was left alone with the other guard – nice fella by the name of Bell. Billy asked Bell to take him down to the latrine, which was outside. When he came back Billy went up the stairs as fast as his leg irons would let him an' at the top of the stairs, instead of turnin' into the room which was his prison, he flattened himself against the wall.

"Now Billy had very small hands, they were more like a girl's. He managed to slip his handcuffs off, quite easy. An' as Bell reached the upper floor Billy just snatched the gun out of his holster. Bell turned and ran

15

down the stairs. Billy fired once an', I guess, missed on purpose. He shouted to Bell to stop as he didn't wanna shoot him, but Bell kept on runnin' so Billy killed him. The bullet caught him in the left shoulder over the heart. He staggered into the yard and fell dead.

"Across the street in the hotel Ollinger heard the shots. He yelled: 'By God, Bell has killed the Kid,' and ran across the road. At the corner of the courthouse he heard the voice of Billy sayin': 'Hello, Bob.'

"He looked up and there was Billy the Kid, holdin' his own shotgun. After the way Ollinger had taunted him, I guess Billy enjoyed pullin' the trigger. Ollinger got the first charge full in the chest. He fell down and Billy gave him the second barrel. By now there was a pretty big crowd in the street. Billy didn't take any notice. He shouted to the handyman: 'Get me a file and throw it up on the porch in front. Then go to the corral and saddle a horse. And leave it ground-hitched just below.' Then as cool as ice he went to the armoury and got himself a rifle and a belt of cartridges. Then he hobbled out on to the porch. I was with the crowd on the other side of the street and I saw him sit down with his rifle across his knees. He took a file from the handyman and began to rasp away at the chain that held his leg irons.

"It was a strange thing, there were several *hombres* in the crowd who owed a grudge to Billy, and I guess he would have been a sittin' duck for anyone who wanted to take a shot at him, yet nobody moved. The only noise was the scrape of the file. The minutes went by and Billy sawed at the chain until it parted. He stood up and did a sorta war dance. I guess he'd been hobbled so long his legs were stiff and he wanted to get his muscles workin' again.

"Then he came down into the street and climbed into the saddle of the horse the handyman had brought round. Still nobody said a word. The Kid looked round at the crowd, sort of raised his hand and said: '*Hasta la vista.*' And he trotted out of town towards the west."

Sam Cash passed the bottle back to Royle. "Not long after that," he continued, "I heard how Pat Garrett, once a friend of the Kid, shot down Billy when he was unarmed. The strange thing was that the gun Garrett used was Wild Bill Hickok's Peacemaker. Wild Bill's sister had given it to Garrett after her brother had been shot through the back of the head by Jack McCall while he was playing poker in Deadwood. An' you know, when they took the cards from his hand, he had aces and eights – the deadman's hand!"

"Yep, sure a strange story," said Royle. "I've a brother that does a bit of preachin'. He was always quotin' at me: 'They who live by the Colt shall die by the Colt'."

For a while the two men rested in the shade, passing the bottle between them. Then Sam Cash said: "The Kid's great speciality with the gun was lighting matches. Like to have a try?"

Royle looked up at Cash who had now climbed to his feet and was stretching himself. It was obvious that here was a man who was obsessed by guns and gunplay. From the one or two hints he'd dropped, he might even owe his livelihood to the 'hardware from Hartford' he wore low down on his thigh, the fancy holster held tight against his leg by a leather thong.

"I'm game to have a try," Royle said. "Shall we make it interestin'?"

"As you like," said Sam Cash. "What are you willin' to put up?"

"Anythin' except my horse and my gun," said Royle.

"Is that a watch you've got on the end of that chain?" asked Sam Cash. Royle nodded. "Sure could use a watch. Will you stake your timepiece?"

"Sure thing. An' I'll ask you to put up them fancy

Mexican spurs of yourn."

"Now I sure would hate to lose them spurs. But I guess it's your timepiece against my spurs. Okay?"

"Okay," said Royle. "Plant the matches."

Cash paced over to a clear patch of sand and, with the aid of some stones, packed a row of matches into it. "Best out of six," he said. "Alternative shots. All right by you?"

"All right by me," replied Royle.

Sam Cash walked back and went down on one knee beside Royle. Steadying his right wrist on his left forearm, he took careful aim at the matches. Even at a short distance it was hard to see the tiny white splinters because of the heat shimmer. Royle stood up and extended his right arm to its full length so that the Frontier was held like a pointing finger.

"Ready when you are," he said.

"Right, *compadre*" grinned Sam Cash and pulled the trigger. A fountain of sand sprayed up by the first match. The impact knocked it slightly sideways, but it remained embedded in the sand. Royle fired. The gun bucked in his hand and the echo of the shot went rolling across the plain. His bullet had struck the match and buried it.

"Not bad," commented Sam Cash. "Watch this." He pulled the trigger a second time and his slug sent a match spinning up into the air. Royle followed him, but his bullet went wide, hit a rock and ricochetted into the distance with a high-pitched whine.

"Guess we're about equal," said Sam Cash.

His bullet made a furrow by the next match but it remained standing. Royle rubbed his left hand across his eyes, raised his gun quickly and fired. The matchstick snapped neatly in two. Without a word Sam Cash fired again. The next matchstick in line splintered under the impact of the .45 slug. Royle got his next matchstick and so did Sam Cash.

"Waal, here's my lucky last," said Sam Cash and he fired the sixth bullet in his gun. His aim was true and the match-stick went spinning. "Not bad," he mused. "Guess I'm still not up to Billy the Kid's standard. He used to set the durned things alight."

Royle raised his gun slowly, almost casually. He gently squeezed the trigger. The matchstick trembled, but stayed planted in the sand and from its head there blossomed a small yellow flame.

Without a word Sam Cash sat down and began unbuckling the silver spurs that had been his pride. "If you ever want a job, *compadre*, I know a fella who's looking for men like you," he said as he handed them over to Royle.

"Thanks," Royle said, "but I ain't lookin' for a job with a gun. I'm goin' to Silver Bend to help my brother dig a well."

* * *

The sun was an angry ball of crimson fire when it slipped below the edge of the world. Mauve shadows raced across the plain as night began to fall on the parched land.

"Better make camp," said Sam Cash to Royle, who was riding beside him. The two men turned off the trail and found a small gulch which would make an ideal camping site. In normal times there was probably a small stream running along it, but since the drought had come the land was rapidly turning into a desert. While Sam Cash watered the horses from the canvas water bags which both men carried, Royle knelt down and made a small Indian-style fire which would burn without throwing up flames to warn marauders of their whereabouts.

"I must say your company ain't exactly unacceptable tonight," said Sam Cash. "I've heard tell that in this part of the territory there are several gangs makin' a speciality of waylayin' travellers. They reckon they're *hombres* who've lost their jobs since the drought came, and ain't too particular about what they do."

Soon coffee was boiling over the fire and the men sat down to their evening meal. By the time they were rolling their last cigarettes for the day the sky was black velvet sprinkled with stars glittering like crushed crystal. A warm drought wind sighed across the range.

Royle pulled a blanket over himself and, using his saddle as a pillow, prepared to sleep.

"Goodnight," he called to Sam Cash who was laying out his blanket on the other side of the camp fire.

"*Buenos noches, compadre.*"

Royle never knew what woke him. It might have been the snap of a twig or the chink of a stone. He opened his eyes slowly. He saw the full moon riding high, telling him that he had been asleep for several hours. Without stirring his body, his eyes swivelled across the embers of the fire to the outline of Sam Cash in his blankets. There he saw a dark figure in the moonlight, a gleaming bowie knife in his raised hand. Soundlessly Royle's hand snaked to where the Frontier was hidden under the arch of his saddle, but before he could find it the bowie knife flashed down, transfixing the bundle that was his sleeping companion.

"Good work," hissed an unseen voice. "He never made a sound. I'll get this one."

Royle turned his head to see another man standing above him, an axe poised to swing. It was an agonising moment. His hand touched the butt of his gun, but he knew he would not have time to bring it out before the blade came arcing down. He tried to roll sideways but the blanket caught him.

Somewhere there was a shot. The man with the axe gave a little moan. The weapon fell from his fingers, the head cleaving the earth beside Royle's head. Then slowly, slowly the assailant crumpled to the ground.

The man with the bowie stood for a moment, bewildered, looking first at his victim and then over at his friend. Royle sat up and fired. The Frontier bullet caught the night raider in the shoulder and its impact spun him. With a howl of pain he turned and ran into the shadows of the mesquite. Seconds later came the muffled drumming of hooves. By then Royle was bending over the bundle by the ashes of the camp fire from which protruded grotesquely the handle of the bowie knife.

He grabbed at the blankets – and realised they did not contain the body of his friend but a log which Sam Cash had used as a decoy. He gave a laugh of relief. In the short time he had known Sam Cash he had got to like the bearded gunman.

"It always pays to sleep in two places at once," said Sam Cash, walking out of the shadows. Without a word Royle sat down on the dummy. Like most Westerners he had a fear of snakes, and he always slept out on the range with his boots on. Now he undid the straps of the silver spurs. These he handed back to Sam Cash.

"Guess that evens the score," he grinned. "If it hadn't been for your shot, I'd have been lyin' there with an axe in my skull."

Sam Cash smiled with delight to get the spurs back, although he drawled modestly, "Just a lucky shot, I guess."

They walked over to the sprawled body of the would-be assassin. Unconcernedly, Sam Cash bent down, grabbed an ankle and dragged the body away into a patch of sagebrush.

"Guess the drought won't worry him no more," he said.

CHAPTER 3

The town of Silver Bend was made up of a single long street of clapboard buildings. A few of these were two-storeys high. The remainder pretended they were by use of false fronts which fooled nobody. In the winter carts some-times got stuck axle-deep in the mud of the street. In the summer the thoroughfare, which rejoiced in the name of Main Street, had the texture of a desert.

The town had gained its name some years back when it was hoped by some over-optimistic prospectors that it would be the site of a silver lode. For a while they believed Silver Bend would be a second Tombstone but the only mineral of value ever taken from the surrounding diggings had been carefully planted there by ingenious individuals who used this method of 'salting' to attract greenhorns with more money than experience.

After the prospectors moved out, chasing a rumour that gold had been found to the south, the smallholders had moved in and made Silver Bend their headquarters. And yet, although the ranchers were a trifle more peaceable than the prospectors, Silver Bend retained something of the brawling atmosphere of a mining town. At the east end was the Good Luck Saloon which had become the centre for the smallholders. At the west end was the optimistically titled Silver Lode, the place of recreation for the hard-riding punchers of the giant Circle-Star ranch.

The patrons of the Silver Lode and the Good Luck had very little to do with each other, apart from feeling resentment. Sometimes they would meet in the mutual territory of the Red Light dance hall and this was when fights broke out. Then in his small office-cum-jailhouse,

Marshal Dolan would lay aside his whisky bottle, regretfully pin on his five-pointed star and, with a shotgun dangerously cradled in his arms, weave his way in the direction of the disturbance, hopeful that it would have sorted itself out by the time he reached it.

On the Sunday that Royle and Sam Cash rode into Silver Bend, miniature dust devils were spinning down the street. The trail companions tied their horses to a hitching rail before going in search of a parting drink. As they walked stiff-legged along the boardwalk under the continuous veranda that fronted the unpainted buildings, they saw a crowd of citizens had collected along the street. A speaker was addressing them from the height of a buckboard and it was clear that a Sunday gospel gathering was in progress. As Silver Bend did not boast a meeting hall, the spreading of the Good Word had to be done in the open.

As they approached on the other side of the street, the two men paused in the shade to listen to the preacher. He seemed to be well into his subject, and whenever he made a point that struck a chord with his audience several enthusiasts would respond with a spirited "Hallelujah", or "Amen to all that."

"Now, Brethren," he was saying, "I want to ask you a question. Why is it that we have been afflicted with this here drought?"

"Because there ain't been any rain," called a humorist from the outskirts of the throng.

"I'll tell you why we've been afflicted with this here drought," the preacher thundered, ignoring the heckler. "It's because we deserve drought – There's been too much takin' of hard waters, too much interest in games of chance and too many fellas fallin' for the false wiles of scarlet women."

Here he gestured in disgust in the general direction of the Red Light dance hall.

"Whores of Babylon!" cried a be-whiskered, be-whiskied gentleman, proud of his Biblical knowledge.

"In Silver Bend," the preacher continued, "Men walk around with the instruments of death strapped to their thighs. They shoot each other down like dogs, takin' the law unto their own hands. They think, poor critters, they are above divine judgement. And it ain't only in this town, folks. There's some hereabouts who think they have the right of the Almighty. They think they can hold back the waters the Good Lord intended for us all."

"You're durned right there, padre," called somebody in the crowd, and the expert on Babylonian immorality was so much in agreement that he discharged his pistol above his head.

"The good Lord sits up there," the preacher went on, unabashed by this agreement. "And he looks down on Silver Bend and on all the wickedness that's goin' on and he says to himself: 'The last time Man was evil, I sent a whole lot of rain. I sent it down for forty days and forty nights. This time I'm gonna teach him another lesson. I'm gonna hold back the rain.'

"Oh yes, my brothers, this drought is gonna last until there's some mighty big changes made round here. There's a lot of prayin' to be done, and a lot of you are gonna have to mend your ways before the clouds roll up and the lightning flashes an' you feel the rain of heaven on your faces. On your knees an' pray, you boozin', gamblin', petticoat-chasin' varmints ...'

"You know," said Sam Cash to Royle in the background, "there's something funny about that sky pilot. He looks like you."

"I should say," Royle said. "He's my brother."

"Well, I'll be durned," said Sam Cash. "Fancy, an ornery gunslinger like you with a Bible-banger for a brother."

"That's what worries him, too," said Royle. His

face smiled but his eyes remained bleak. "Let's go an' get outside that drink."

"Ain't you going to go up and say howdy to your brother?"

"No, that can wait. I'd hate to bust up his meetin'. He's going like a riverboat with a full head of steam now."

As the two men continued on their way they heard the loud throb of a drum from the opposite end of Silver Bend.

"It sounds like brother Ethan's got some opposition," Royle laughed. "Let's go and see what this is about."

"This sure seems a lively little town," grinned Sam Cash. He added: "An' I've got a hunch it's gonna be a lot livelier soon."

Royle looked sideways at his companion. "I know drought makes people kind of edgy," he said. "But Silver Bend ain't Lincoln, Sam, if that's what you're thinkin' on."

"Who said anything about Lincoln County?" said Sam innocently. "Come on, let's see what that drum-beatin's all about."

At the far end of Main Street, a covered wagon was standing opposite the Good Luck Saloon. Oxen stood patiently on either side of its long pole, but it was not the kind of prairie schooner in which emigrants had come from the East to find a new land. It was more like a circus wagon, its canvas was bright yellow and this formed a background for letters in vivid scarlet which proclaimed: JONATHAN Q. NIMROD, RAINMAKER.

On the platform by the driver's seat stood a large, portly man solemnly beating the drum which rested comically on his corpulence. His face was an impressive red, a hue caused more by application to the whisky bottle than the rays of the sun. From under his white Stetson flowed locks of snowy hair. He wore a slightly shabby but elegantly cut frockcoat and when he finally put the drum down there were whistles of admiration at the glowing pattern of his waistcoat.

It had not taken him long to drum up a large audience, and looking down the road Royle saw his brother had been deserted except for a handful of the most devoted members of his flock. Even the men from the Good Luck Saloon had come out and stood on the veranda, glasses in their hands. When the owner of the wagon saw that he had most of the population before him, he made a flamboyant bow and said, in a surprisingly deep voice: "Citizens of this fair city of Silver Bend, allow me to introduce myself. I am, as you can see from the name inscribed on this here wagon, Jonathan Q. Nimrod."

At this information there were some ironical cheers.

"And furthermore," continued Jonathan Q. Nimrod, "I am a rainmaker. Now let's get this straight right away, folks. I am not here to do the three card trick or to sell you wooden dimes or peddle snake oil cures. No, sirree. I am a man of science and I have come to help you in your hour of need. And by the look of things around here, folks, you need my help. As I came through the territory in my wagon, I saw how your grass had withered, an' I saw your steers with their bones damn near sticking out through their miserable hides. I said to myself, Jonathan Nimrod, Silver Bend needs you. Yes, friends, I am here to help. I do not do it through conjurin'. I do it through scientific principles I have worked out through studyin' at the universities of Europe. Lemme explain. Rain is made up of water and water is a chemical, and therefore water must respond to the laws of chemistry. And after years of patient study I've found what them laws are, and I can control water so that it will droppeth like the gentle dew of heaven.

"Why am I so confident in my claims, you may ask. The answer, friends, is because I have done it before.

"Say, did you ever hear about the dry spell they had over at Bitter Creek three years back? They had the drought pretty bad there. When I was called in to that little town, I found half the citizens on their knees praying for rain and the other half trying to prove they could do without it by the use of alcohol. I set up my equipment, and I sent my chemical smoke high into the sky and before long great black clouds started to form. Suddenly the lightning flashed, and the rain started to come down and I knew that I wouldn't be needed in Bitter Creek any more. So I harnessed up and away I went and all the next day the rain came tumbling down. Finally a posse caught me up and pointed their guns at me. They were men from Bitter Creek. So I said: 'What's this, friends, why are you pointing guns at me? I am the man who saved you from ruin.' 'You come right back to Bitter Creek,' they said, 'and stop the goshdarned rain. Right now half the town's washed away with the flood.'

There was a ripple of amusement at the story. Jonathan Q. Nimrod raised his hands to quell the laughter and then continued on a more serious note.

"Now, citizens of Silver Bend, I can do for you what I did for the citizens of Bitter Creek."

"I guess he sure can at that, neighbours," cried a man in the crowd suddenly. "I heard tell of him before." All eyes swivelled to the speaker. He was a man who had only recently arrived at Silver Bend and, as was ascertained afterwards, had come as a stooge for the rainmaker. "Yes, sirree," he continued, "I heard of him when I was over in the Stone Forest country. He brought the rain all right when they was all parched up. They still talk about him over there."

This confirmation electrified the onlookers. They

27

looked back at the figure standing on the wagon. Now there was respect on some faces, and on some – hope.

"Would you mind tellin' us, mister, just how you would go about bringin' the rain?" asked Marshal Dolan from the veranda of the Good Luck Saloon.

"Certainly, sir. I see from that star you wear that you are the representative of justice and of the citizens of this fair town. So I shall be happy to tell you, sir, and look upon you as their leader. It amounts to this. I've found, through years of scientific study, that by mixin' certain chemicals together in a secret way, and sendin' the smoke from these aforesaid chemicals into the sky, it will cause rain clouds to form. 'Course, I have to keep my methods to myself. Wouldn't do if everyone knew how to make rain. I guess if they did, most of the United States would be washed away by now.

"Folks, I'm willin' to make your grass green again, to make your cattle fat, to make your wives smile, by causing the heavens to open an' the rain to fall. But the chemicals I have to burn are mighty, mighty costly. And therefore I have to ask for a fee."

There was a solemn silence, then the marshal inquired: "What might that be, sir?"

"The cost of bringin' down rain," Jonathan Q. Nimrod said, "is one thousand United States dollars, cash. I say cash because I have had the regrettable experience that once the rain comes down, folk ain't half so keen to shell out. So I gotta be business-like."

"Trouble is, that – er – I guess there ain't anybody here with a thousand dollars," a smallholder said. "Since the drought come we've lost so much money, I guess most of us only got a few dollars left."

"Ah, that is a situation I do appreciate, sir," said the rainmaker. "But I wouldn't expect any single man to pay me a thousand dollars. No, sir, everybody benefits from the rain so everybody ought to ante up. If you want me to bring down the rain, everybody here should put what they can in a fund. Maybe our good friend the marshal might look after it for us. Make sure everythin' is fair an' square. And when that fund reaches the sum of a thousand dollars, I shall build my towers and light my fires and leave the rest up to Science. I ain't goin' to talk any more, friends. I've told you what I can do for you, the rest is up to you. I'm gonna be here a day or two before I move on, to alleviate drought in other parts. Meanwhile I'm gonna have a drink 'cause my throat's got as dry as your pastures with talkin'."

The bulky man climbed down from his wagon and walked through the crowd to the bat-wing doors of the Good Luck Saloon. Here he turned. "As a gesture of good faith, friends," he said, "the first round is on me."

Instantly there was a cheer and a rush for the saloon. "Come on," drawled Sam Cash as he and Royle followed the crowd into the bar. "I guess maybe you won't be diggin' that well after all."

On the wall above the long bar of the Good Luck Saloon, Royle saw a scrawled notice which read: *Tonite Silver Bend Cattlemen's Protection Association meeting.* Under it was scrawled: *Join the fight for your water right.*

For a while the two men who had shared part of the trail to Silver Bend said nothing, listening to the hubbub of conversation that was going on all around them. Some were arguing the merits of rainmaking, others were cursing the Circle-Star ranch and Boss Quinn in particular for depriving them of water.

"If he ain't careful, Boss Quinn will have a war on his hands sure as hell," said a man to the left of Royle.

"I guess he expects that," said another. "I've heard tell he's bringin' in some hired guns for extra protection."

"A lot of good that'll do him," said a third. "If we got organised we could ride over there and blow his dam to Kingdom Come."

Suddenly a voice cut through the conversation: "Talking of hired guns, boys, look what we've got here."

Royle turned round so that his back was to the bar. He saw a burly, belly-sagging man with a big, red moustache and red hair. There was a fuzz of ginger hair on his mottled arms. His name was Hyatt, and he was pointing at Royle's companion, whose face he recognised in the mirror at the back of the bar.

"Look, boys," he drawled. "If it ain't Sam Cash. Last time I saw him he was carryin' a gun for the Lincoln County cattle barons. I'd take a little bet he's come to do the same for Boss Quinn."

The noise in the bar had withered away to a silence. Slowly Sam Cash turned around to face the big man.

"Are you makin' them remarks about me, friend?" he said in a voice that had gone dangerously silky.

"I was," replied Hyatt. "I was sayin', Sam Cash, you was totin' a gun in the Lincoln County war, an' I guess you're here to do the same here–only the war ain't quite started yet."

"Look, *compadre*," said Sam Cash, insolently tipping his hat brim down over his eyes, "I ain't got no quarrel with you, so don't tread on your luck. I've come here to work for Boss Quinn as a rangerider. There ain't nothin' more to it than that."

"Isn't there?" said the big man. "There's several of us fellas in Silver Bend who had to move outa Lincoln County because of your kind. Keep your eyes open. Maybe someone will repay an old score."

Sam Cash gave an exaggerated shrug but his right hand remained near the butt of his pistol. "I guess that's my problem, but if you've got any evenin' up to do I guess this is quite a good time and place to do it."

The big man flushed, suddenly aware that he could be facing death in the form of the dark stranger, lounging

30

against the bar in front of him.

"Well, *compadre*," smiled Sam Cash. "You've gone doggone quiet all of a sudden."

Royle was conscious of the tension mounting in the packed saloon. The silence was suddenly so complete he was vividly aware of the buzzing of a fly, of a few indistinct wind-borne words floating through the window from his brother's meeting. Everyone knew that within seconds there was a chance they would see guns leap from holsters, and that one of the two men could be sprawled on the floor under a pall of a black cloud of smoke. Then the stillness was shattered by the slurring voice of Marshal Dolan.

"Goshdarn it, boys," he complained. "Don't give me no trouble this Sunday mornin'. One of you might miss and hit the rainmaker here. Then where would we be?"

There was a roar of laughter. It was not that the joke was funny. It was the laughter of relief. The only man who didn't grin was Sam Cash. Royle saw there was a strange glitter in his eyes, and his lips were drawn back in a wolfish grimace of anticipation. Royle realised Cash was disappointed that the other man had not gone for his gun.

He had been eager for that split-second moment of deadly action and the strange, perverted joy of the gunman in seeing someone die by the skill of his shooting. Buried in this man, so pleasant in many respects, was an obsession with death.

Hyatt mumbled something and turned away. The crowd swept back to the bar, but now conversations were muted and there were many glances in the direction of Sam Cash.

"Come on, Sam," said Royle. "I've gotta get along and I guess you have, too."

Cash turned to him looking as though he were

31

coming out of a daze. "Yep," he said. "Let's get on our way."

He walked to the door of the saloon and then turned and faced the company. "If any of you fellas here think you have a grudge to settle from way back," he said in tones of ice, "an' you feel you wanna do somethin' about it – well, I won't be hard to find."

As the two companions left the saloon and started down the road, there was a crash of swing doors and a voice cried, "Hands up, Cash, you varmint, or I'll let daylight right through you."

Royle spun round to see Hyatt, armed with the barman's scattergun. The deadly weapon pointed remorselessly at the small of Cash's back. Instinctively aware of the danger, Sam Cash began to raise his arms without looking around. At that moment, Royle's gun sounded. The scattergun jerked out of Hyatt's hand, exploded harmlessly into the ground, and from his throat was torn a curse of agony. Blood began to ooze among the reddish hairs on either side of the painful crease the Frontier's bullet had cut across his forearm.

"Don't get ideas about goin' for your sixgun," Royle snapped. "The next bullet might not be so considerate."

"Goddam you both to hell," snarled Hyatt as his friends led him back into the saloon.

Neither Royle nor Cash spoke until they reached their horses. Then, "Thanks very much," said Cash.

"Forget it," Royle said. "I was only repayin' the compliment."

"Even so, *compadre*," said Cash, "I'd like you to have these as a sorta keepsake." Bending down, he unbuckled the silver spurs which he tossed to Royle. "*Hasta la vista*" he cried, swung into the saddle and cantered off along the trail that led to the Circle-Star.

CHAPTER 4

"Pretty little place you've got," remarked Royle to his brother, Ethan, as the two men approached a small, white-washed house surrounded by fruit trees and a vegetable garden which, on account of the drought, now only boasted a few withered stalks.

"The Lord provided for us well," said Ethan, as he led the way round to the corral at the back of the house. "Three years ago we came here and I built this house. And they were fruitful years till the drought came. Even now, I ain't so bad off as many. My creek ain't wholly dried up yet. It's the ones further away from The Plateau that have suffered most."

"From what I heard back in Silver Bend, there's sure a lot of feelin' against the Circle-Star 'cause of the dam across the Snowy River."

"That's so," said Ethan. "They created themselves a lake there an' drive their herds down to water regular. Makes the small ranchers hereabouts pretty bitter to think of all that water there, because even without rain the river won't go completely dry, seein' how it's fed from Mount Snowy."

"Waal, there's an answer to that," Royle said as he bent to unbuckle his girth-strap.

"What's that?" asked Ethan.

"Blastin' powder."

"I was afraid that's the sort of answer you'd give, Lee. I can see you're still a man of wrath. Even this morning you had to use that accursed gun of yours."

"My accursed gun saved a guy's life," Royle said mildly. "An', Ethan, I'd like to say the past is the past, and there ain't no point in talkin' about it. Let's say I've paid the penalty anyway. But I still hate to see folk pushin' other folk around. I used my gun this mornin' 'cause a half-drunk coward with a grudge aimed a scattergun at the back of a man who saved my life on the trail. So I grazed the arm of this coyote – it's only a light wound, it'll heal in a few days. I coulda shot him stone dead at that range.

"As for the dam – if I had a smallholdin' an' saw my cattle dyin', I'd sure go and plant some blastin' powder under it. A man's got a right to what's his own an' no one can put a brand on water.

"Still, don't worry, brother, I ain't lookin' for trouble. All I want is to dig your well and maybe mosey round the range a bit. For the last few years I've been dreamin' of just sittin' on a cayuse an' ridin' wherever I please."

"Our ways are very different, Lee," said Ethan. "But we have the same blood in our veins, and it won't do to quarrel none. It don't matter that we don't think alike, you are always welcome here. Now come an' meet Linda. She's still as pretty as a picture."

A brief look of anxiety flickered in the faded eyes of Royle, but his brother didn't notice. Already he was leading the way along the little path to the kitchen door of the house. Inside the kitchen a young woman in a pale blue gingham dress stood over a black iron stove. At first Royle could only see her back, with the long braid of golden hair, tied in a ribbon, hanging almost down to her waist. Hearing the footsteps of the men, she turned. Her eyes widened when she saw Royle following her husband.

"The prodigal has returned," said Ethan in high humour. "Linda, I guess it's time to kill the fatted calf."

"Hello, Linda," murmured Royle, standing by the door, his black hat held politely in his hand.

"Hello, Lee," replied Linda, her voice with a note of tension in it. "Welcome to our home."

"I'll just go out and see about gettin' them two

poor hosses their water ration," said Ethan. As he left the kitchen Linda walked up to Lee. Gravely she put her hands on his shoulders and kissed him hard on the mouth. Then she stepped back and looked into his face searchingly. "Why have you come, Lee?" she asked. "Because of this," Royle said, and he pulled a crumpled letter from his pocket. "Ethan wrote an' asked me to come and help him dig a well. You must have knowed that. Funnily enough, one of the things I'm good at is well-diggin'. I found out I'm a dowser. By the look of things around here a well would be a mighty useful thing to have."

"Lee," said Linda. "I want you to know one thing. I'm a good wife to your brother. I want it to stay that way."

Royle looked around the kitchen and through the door that led into the comfortable living-room. "I can see you're a good wife, Linda," he said with a bleak smile. "An' don't worry about me. The past is the past, as I was sayin' to Ethan. Things change, people change – an' you can never go back. So just look on me as your brother-in-law, and forget that before my trouble there was anything –"

"Maybe it's easy for you to say," said Linda, suddenly fierce. "Of course people can't go back in time, but they can't not remember either. Sometimes when I've looked at Ethan–it must be some trick of the light – I thought I've seen your face. For a moment I've hated him for remindin' me."

For a while neither said anything. Linda busied herself making a pot of coffee on the stove. To cover the awkwardness Royle went outside and brought in some chopped-up stove wood for her.

"I see you still carry a gun," she said as he laid the load by the stove.

"Yep," Royle said. "I still carry a gun. But I ain't

35

any more anxious to use it now than I used to be."

"How you talk," said Linda suddenly laughing. "Trying to make out you are all reformed. You'll be going along speaking at Ethan's meeting soon."

It was Royle's turn to laugh. "I can't exactly see myself doin' that, Linda. But from what I saw this mornin' in Silver Bend he sure is pretty good when it comes to layin' down the Good Word."

"I know. He's a fine man. This country needs more men like him. Very strange that you two should be brothers. You look alike and yet you're so different. It's as though Ethan got your share of gentleness – an' you got his share of violence."

Royle smiled slightly, looking with approving eyes at his sister-in-law.

"You still make mighty good coffee, Linda," he said. "For the last few years I used to think about your coffee – among other things I used to think about you."

"Was it bad? Did they treat you bad?" Royle shrugged. "It's always bad not to be free. But they didn't treat me mean – not on purpose, anyways. After a while they let me go outside to work. An' that's where I learnt to do well-diggin'. There's a sight more to well-diggin' than just making a hole in the ground."

"What's this about well-digging?" asked Ethan, coming through the door. "D'you reckon you'll be able to find water here?"

"Probably," said Royle. "There's water most places if you go down deep enough. After we've eaten I'd better go an' do some dowsin'."

"Not today, you won't," said Ethan. "It's the Sabbath. We'll start work tomorrow." "Okay by me," said Royle.

There was the sound of horses' hooves, then the creak of leather as a rider dismounted. The two brothers walked outside to see who the visitor might be. Linda looked from the open kitchen window.

Royle saw a narrow-hipped man in his mid-thirties standing on the path. From under his black sombrero a lock of black hair hung down over his forehead. His face was thin and high cheek-boned. He wore a narrow, black moustache and a short pointed beard which gave his swarthy features the look of a Spanish grandee. A black silk kerchief was knotted round his neck and his shirt and trousers were of the same colour.

The first thing Royle had noticed was that he carried two guns,, and wore the holsters high over his hips in such a way that the ivory butts faced inwards indicating his method of gunfighting was to use a cross-draw.

"I've come from Boss Quinn with a message for you, Brother Royle," he said sneeringly to Ethan. "He's heard tell that when you've been preachin' lately you've made certain remarks about a certain dam, an' aired your opinions about water belonging to everybody."

"I sure have," said Ethan. "Some days back I was tellin' him this to his face."

"Waal," drawled the messenger, "don't do it no more. Boss Quinn ain't worried about your opinion, but he figgers what you're saying might stir up some folk to do foolish things. So if you wanna keep healthy, Royle, give up preach-in' for a while. Savvy?"

"Seems to me you're makin' a mighty big threat against a man who doesn't carry a gun," said Royle with deceptive mildness. "I guess your boss must be pretty nervous if he has to send a gunslinger to warn off a preacher." The man's eyes flicked to Royle.

"By the look of you, you must be Lee Royle, the preacher's famous brother," he said in a cold voice. "Don't you get no ideas either, fella. Quite a bit of time has gone by since you were top gun down Sonora way. Things have changed, new men have come along. You still may be able to shoot straight, but there are a lot of

37

guys ready to lay money you ain't anywhere near as fast as you used to be."

"Mebbe we'll find out someday."

The man in black shrugged. "Anyways, that's my message," he said. "Lay off the preaching until the drought breaks." He turned on his heel, swung into the saddle and cantered off, leaving a trail of powdered earth hanging suspended in the hot air behind him.

"An' who was that *hombre*?" asked Royle.

"His name is Pete Montana," said Ethan. "He's Boss Quinn's foreman on the Circle-Star."

"I can see Boss Quinn likes to have some tough fellas on his payroll," said Royle.

"He's an evil man," said Linda.

* * *

Just before sunset Ethan Royle took his brother to Silver Bend on his buckboard. They tied the reins to the Good Luck Saloon hitching rail and went inside. Ethan ordered a mineral water and Lee a beer.

"I see you ain't fallen to the Demon Drink yet," laughed Royle as they found themselves a table in a corner of the saloon. "Maybe if you tried it you'd find out what you've been missin' all these years. Might make a new man out of you."

Ethan looked at his brother with an amused expression. "As long as I'm able to put you down in a fair fist fight I don't need to be a new man," he smiled. "I used to be able to lick you before an' I reckon I still could."

Royle regarded the lean figure opposite. "I still reckon you just might be able to do it at that," he conceded.

The garish, be-mirrored saloon was full of ranchers and smallholders waiting for the advertised meeting of the Silver Bend Cattlemen's Protection Association. At a table near the bar Marshal Dolan was collecting donations towards the rainmaker's fund. As men walked up and pushed over their little piles of coins he carefully entered the amount on a piece of paper and, drawing inspiration from a bottle at his elbow, would harangue the assembly: "Come on, fellas, some of you guys ain't shelled out yet, an' I know darned well some of you could part up with a lot more. I reckon our best chance of beatin' the drought is with this here scientific fella. If the rains come it'll be worth every cent of a thousand dollars."

"What's your percentage, Marshal?" laughed someone at the bar.

"Oh, he ain't getting no percentage," came a reply. "It's just that Nimrod fella promised to beat his own personal drought with whisky."

Of Jonathan Q. Nimrod himself there was no sign. It was as though he preferred not to intrude on the sordid question of money.

"Who's behind the Cattlemen's Protection Association?" asked Royle without much curiosity.

"A man by the name of Jason Shepherd. He's got the largest ranch around here, apart from the Circle-Star. He's been pretty hard hit by the drought and he's plenty bitter. Can't say that I blame him. Only hope he ain't gonna try and get this lot of men to take the law into their own hands. That won't solve anythin'."

Suddenly there was a hammering on the bar with the butt of a six-shooter. The laughter and conversation died away and Jason Shepherd, a man with thinning hair and a spade beard, thrust his gun back into the holster and began to address the meeting.

"Neighbours," he said in an authoritative voice, "you all know the reason we're here tonight. It's because of the drought. Unless we get water in the next two or three weeks the creeks'll be dry an' we'll be out of business. Now we all know, and Brother Royle over there should agree with me, that drought is an act of God, but the Lord helps them that helps themselves, an' in this case there are several things we could try. For one thing you can walk up, give your dollar to Marshal Dolan and maybe the conjure man we saw this afternoon will send some smoke up into the sky and it'll rain. Maybe. The other thing we can do is get rid of that goddarned dam that's holding back what's rightfully ours."

There was a mutter of agreement at this. "Now, neighbours, I move that the Silver Bend Cattlemen's Protection Association looks into the ways and means of gettin' rid of the dam Boss Quinn has thrown across the river – an' I'd like to hear if you've got any suggestions." There was a buzz of agreement. A score of conversations started. Jason Shepherd banged on the bar again so that the glasses jumped.

"Now, neighbours, let's have some order," he demanded. "Has anyone got anythin' they'd like to contribute towards this here meetin'?"

For some seconds the men looked at each other's faces, each waiting for the first one to get up and speak. Then Ethan Royle climbed to his feet.

"Friends," he said, "tonight I ain't gonna preach to you no sermon. Like yourselves I got a small bit of land here and everything I own depends on getting the Good Lord's water just the same as the rest of you. You may think that because I do a bit o' preachin' I'm not a practical man. Well, that ain't so and like most of you here I reckon that it was wrong to throw a dam across the Snowy River. Like most of you here I think we ought to get rid of that dam. But what I also think is that you'll never get rid of it by force. It's gotta be done proper and legal. So I move that we send a telegraph message to Congress an' ask them to send militia to let the water through. In my pocket here I got a draft for the message I think we ought to send, warnin' the Government that unless action is taken there'll be trouble." He sat down

40

again.

The following speakers wrangled backwards and forwards over Ethan Royle's proposal. Some believed that members of Congress, so many hundreds of miles away in Washington, wouldn't be interested in the plight of Silver Bend. At the most it would be referred to the State Governor who would probably side with Boss Quinn. Others said that if the militia were called in by the time they arrived on the scene it would be too late. Another group were all for sending the telegram.

After a lot of argument, Jason Shepherd took the floor again.

"Well, neighbours," he said, "I guess we've got the meat off the bones of all the arguments here. Now what I suggest is this. It can't do no harm to send a telegraph message an' if we don't get a reply within a week I guess we'll know what to do. I move we send the message over to Carsonville where they got a telegraph."

A haggard-faced man rose by the door of the saloon. "Jason," he said. "It durn well won't do. My section of the creek dried up today. Half my beeves are staggering already. In a week's time, my herd'll be gone. I reckon we ought to ride out there tonight."

To his own surprise, Royle found himself climbing to his feet. "I know how you must feel," he said. "But remember this. There's one thing worse than seeing your beeves die and that's gettin' a bellyful of lead. From what I've got my loop round in the short time I've been here this man Boss Quinn has been gettin' together a hard bunch of gunmen to protect him. This very mornin' I rode into town with Sam Cash, who's taken a job on the Circle-Star. He's a fine fella but he ain't an ordinary cowpoke. An' then there's Pete Montana, an old-fashioned two-gun man – It's easy talkin' to say 'let's bust the Circle-Star dam', but I reckon if any of you tried it, nobody'd even reach it alive."

41

His words were received in stony silence. He felt he was making a fool of himself, and sat down without another word.

"Well, I guess that ends the meeting," said Jason Shepherd. "We'll send off that there telegraph as Brother Royle suggested, but if any of you feel there's a need for more direct action, I'd like you to stay behind with me an' we'll form a special committee of – uh – ways and means."

"I sure was surprised when you got up and spoke like that, Lee," said Ethan Royle as the buckboard bounced along the track in the bright moonlight towards the small white ranch house. Royle drew on the butt of a cigarette he had been smoking, then carefully stubbed it out against the high heel of his boot. Normally he would have flicked it to one side but this was a time of drought and the withered, tinder-dry vegetation on either side of the trail was ever ready to burst into a sheet of flame.

"I was a bit surprised myself," he admitted.

"I'd thought you'd be on the side of the fellas who wanted to raid the dam," continued Ethan.

"Let's say I changed a bit since you last saw me," said Royle, and they continued the journey in silence.

* * *

The next day Royle rose with the sun. He went out to Ethan's barn and from one of his saddle bags he took a coil of copper wire. This he straightened out until it was six feet long and then bent it into a U shape. Taking it with him, he selected a spot near the front door of the ranch house and, holding an end of the U in each hand, he extended his arms and slowly walked around the house.

When he was level with the kitchen window, Linda called out: "Lee, what on earth are you doing?"

"I'm dowsin'," he grinned. "When I walk over a spring, deep down in the earth, this piece of wire will tip downwards."

"Sounds like the sort of thing the rainmaker in Silver Bend would do," laughed Linda.

"We'll see about that," muttered Lee and continued on his walk. Soon he was joined by his brother in mud stained overalls. He had been endeavouring to get buckets of water from the trickle that ran along the bed of his creek. Pausing only to gulp down some coffee for breakfast, the two men continued to walk round the house in widening circles. As the sun hoisted itself higher into the cloudless sky the sweat trickled down their faces and Royle's arms ached from holding up the copper wire in front of him. It was at midday, at a point about six hundred yards north of the house, when the copper wire began to vibrate.

"I think I've got something, Ethan," Royle said. He paused, then took a step forward. The copper wire, as though it had suddenly gained a life of its own, trembled more violently and then began to point downwards.

"This is it!" cried Royle. He screwed his heel into the powdery earth to mark the exact spot. "Now, let's get shovels and start diggin'. I tell you what, while I start work you bring up all the timber you can get. We'll need it for shorin' up. Somethin' tells me this is gonna be a deep one."

Despite the heat the two men ran back to the farm. Ethan began collecting tools and selecting lengths of timber, while Lee grabbed a long-handled shovel and raced back to the spot. Pausing only to throw off his shirt, he began to dig as though his life depended upon it. The sweat glistened on his body as shovelfuls of soil went flying over his shoulder and he was thankful when Linda approached with a pannikin of water. For a while she regarded his lean body as he worked without speaking. When she finally spoke, she said: "Wouldn't you find it easier to work without that gun hang-in' on your hip?"

Royle drained the pannikin and wiped his mouth on the back of his hand. He looked her straight in the face and said: "If I was going to take this gun off, I guess I shoulda taken it off a long time back."

Without another word he spat on his hands, seized the shovel again and began digging as though he had a personal grudge against the earth he was excavating.

CHAPTER 5

In Silver Bend the days passed with agonising slowness. With drought there is nothing one can do except wait, and the men affected had already learnt to do this. Some, who could not face the look of anxiety in their wives' faces, spent most of their time in Silver Bend, usually at the Good Luck Saloon where they drank heavily and muttered curses about the drought in general and Boss Quinn in particular. They were grateful for any new happening which gave them something to gossip about, something that would take them out of their half-dream state of waiting for the rains that never came.

The first conversation topic was Jonathan Q. Nimrod. As yet the funds for his services had not reached the required amount. At the moment he took his ease on the veranda of Silver Bend's only hotel. His yellow wagon containing the apparatus for his rainmaking experiments was at the local livery stable, but the imposing presence of the rainmaker was enough to keep the question of his services very much alive in the minds of the citizens. The news of his offer had spread abroad and even the wives were coming in from outlying holdings to walk into Marshal Dolan's office and lay down their pathetic savings.

The other topic which was thoroughly discussed at the Good Luck was the Royle brothers. Firstly, it was known that they were attempting to dig a well. The majority had no faith in the operation for they considered that even if there were underground springs they would be dried up on account of the drought. One or two thought it was a good idea and announced that they were going to start digging themselves, right the next day. But somehow

45

the next day didn't come.

The other interesting thing about the Royles was the rumour that Montana, Boss Quinn's foreman, had warned Ethan over preaching about the drought. Bets were being laid as to whether Brother Ethan would brave the threat of the cattle baron and take up his usual stand the following Sunday. And there was some mystery about his brother, Lee, who had already shown that he was not unfamiliar with gunplay. His name rang a distant bell in the memories of several of the Good Luck customers, but it was connected with something that had happened years ago – anyway it was hard to think of the preacher having a brother who once had a gun fighting reputation.

A man who did not enter into the sporadic conversations around the bar was Eddy, the man who had demanded action against Boss Quinn at the meeting of the Silver Bend Cattlemen's Protection Association on the previous Sunday night. He sat at a back table, his head in his hands, and moodily regarded the gradually emptying whisky bottle before him. "'Tain't no use sending telegraphs," he would mutter to himself. "We gotta have action."

Out at the Royle ranch the well-digging was going apace. The square hole was now so deep that one man shovelled at the bottom while the other stood at the top, removing the soil by means of a bucket on a rope. To prevent the earth caving in, baulks of timber had been placed on the sides of the wall and boards had been nailed across them. Since the work had commenced both brothers had toiled at it unsparingly. They started at dawn, worked through until sundown and then carried on in the light of kerosene lamps. By the time they went to bed they would be reeling with fatigue. On the third morning Royle said at the breakfast table: "Think I'll ride into Silver Bend an' order some things we're gonna need. Now that we've got down so deep we want a block and tackle. I could use a new shovel and I guess we'll need some more big nails for shorin' up soon."

"I'll come in with you," said Ethan. "I've got a bit of business to see to."

As they travelled towards the town, Royle riding beside his brother's buckboard, Ethan pointed out the landmarks. To the north was the massive shape of The Plateau, its walls almost dropping sheer to the plain.

"That gap is the entrance to the Circle-Star valley," explained Ethan. "It's through there that what's left of the Snowy River comes. Further up that valley is where Boss Quinn has got his dam. 'Course he owns a lot more than that valley. His territory stretches about ten miles to the north an' he runs his herds on top of The Plateau as well as down in its valleys. An' he's got claim to the land that this trail skirts. He ain't been using it since the drought, though. He's moved the cattle up the valley close to the water supply."

At Silver Bend the brothers parted after making their purchases and loading up the buckboard. It was about noon when Royle started back to the ranch alone. As he left the town he ran the rowels of his spurs – the silver spurs that Sam Cash had given him – over the flank of his horse. He was anxious to get back, anxious to start work again on the well. He felt restless to finish the job and yet he had no idea of what he would do when it was completed, except that he would not stay. Too many memories had flooded back since his arrival.

As he rode he saw that by leaving the trail that bounded the Circle-Star territory, and cutting across within a mile or so of The Plateau walls, he could shorten his journey. The buckboard would have to stick to the path, but there was no need for him to. He left the trail and cantered over the undulating plain.

Sometimes he galloped over areas of dead grass and sometimes his horse was picking his way over dried

47

sage. More and more often he was forcing his way through thickets of mesquite and chaparral. A strong hot wind was blowing from the south, and it was this that brought him the first warning of danger – the pungent odour of burning grass.

He turned in the saddle and looked behind him. A quarter of a mile away he saw a wall of smoke, below which was a thin line of orange. The plain was alight. Royle cursed aloud. He knew that behind him was the most deadly thing on the prairie – a wave of fire that could travel almost as fast as a galloping horse, destroying everything in its speedy wake and leaving only charred trunks of trees like grotesque skeletons and bare smoking earth. He saw the line of fire stretched for at least a mile and was rapidly extending on either side. This meant there was no hope of riding to the east or west and thus getting behind it. The best chance was to ride north and then veer west to get out of the path of the holocaust.

The reek of the fire was now strong in his nostrils and he felt his horse trembling as it sensed the nearness of the greatest enemy of all animals. Royle patted its neck reassuringly and then began riding hard northwards. The wind carried distinctly the roar and crackle of the fire to his ears while from the scrub and sage brush birds cried in alarm and rose flapping into the sky. To his right he saw a Coyote bounding along. Something of its panic fear communicated itself to Royle. His instinct was to spur his horse on as fast as possible but his good sense restrained him. The terrain was rough. He could not see the ground because of the scrub; thorn and sage and he was afraid of his horse putting its hoof into a jack-rabbit hole. He knew that if his horse were brought down his chances would be slim, so he continued with caution, sometimes riding across sandy dried-up water courses, sometimes breasting gentle ridges from where he was able to look back and see the fire. It had now become a vast curve, its smoke blotting out the country behind it, and its leaping line of flame much closer to Royle than when he had first noticed it. At the back of his mind he wondered why the fire should have spread its width so rapidly. It was almost as though it had started at several points simultaneously.

The smoke carried by the wind was growing denser and as the lone rider looked back his eyes smarted. Blackened fragments of burnt foliage whirled past him like charred confetti. As he continued north, sometimes having to curb his mount from blundering into Joshua trees in its terror, he saw a movement to the east. Because of the smoke he could not make out details, but it seemed a large animal was floundering in a patch of mesquite.

Then, during a brief lull in the wind, Royle was able to see a horse plunging and thrashing in agony. Before the curtain of smoke thickened he noticed there was a saddle on its back. Raising his kerchief to cover his mouth and nostrils, he turned in the direction of the riderless mount and, risking the hazards of jack-rabbit holes and hidden rocks, he urged his horse forward with curses and endearments. When he reined up several minutes later he saw at once the cause of the horse's distress. It had broken its left splint bone and now was pitifully trying to escape the blaze behind it.

Sometimes it reared upon its hind legs, neighing in agony, but when it put its weight on the injured foreleg it would lurch forward and fall on its side, thrashing grotesquely and snorting with bewildered pain until it had got upright again. Royle slid the Winchester out of its saddle scabbard. It was hard to take aim. His own horse was restive and rebellious and kept side-stepping under him, its terror increased by the sight of its injured fellow. Royle fired and bit his lip when he saw his first shot had only wounded the unfortunate beast in the neck and added to its agony. He fired again and this time the bullet mercifully found its target between the animal's eyes. It

49

reared for the last time, pawing the air with its good leg, then crashed down with a snapping of undergrowth. It was only then that Royle saw the body of its rider lying nearby.

Royle had to force his mount to carry him over towards the vague shape in a patch of withered grass. As it meant riding towards the fire, the horse kept rearing and Royle had to use Sam Cash's spurs unmercifully to force it on. As he got closer, he saw that it was the body of a young woman. She was wearing a crimson blouse and a long, pleated riding skirt. He swung down from the saddle, and fastened the reins of his horse to a thick stem of a greasewood tree. He unstrapped his water canteen and knelt down by the girl. Her face was unnaturally white, more like a mask of wax and a long strand of blue-black hair had blown across it. For some reason this made Royle think of a broken doll. He poured water on to her face and was reassured to see the rise and fall of her breast. At least she was not dead. With surprising gentleness he ran his fingers through her hair until he encountered a large swelling. It was obvious that when her horse had broken its leg she had been flung from the saddle and been knocked unconscious with the impact.

"Wake up, miss. Wake up, miss," he muttered urgently, glancing over his shoulder. Now he was at ground level he could no longer see the flames, but he could see the clouds of smoke the wind was whipping closer and closer. Above the noise of the conflagration he could hear his horse whickering in terror.

"Wake up, miss – wake up, miss," he implored. A moment later she uttered a moan and her eyes slowly opened.

"My face is all wet," she murmured.

"I'm tryin' to rouse you, miss," Royle said. "You've been thrown from your horse."

From their vacant expression her eyes suddenly

focused on his face. "Who are you?"

"It doesn't matter much at the moment. There's a prairie fire coming our way and we've got to get out of here pronto." The impact of his words seemed to have more effect on her than the water.

"I remember," she gasped. "I was trying to get away when Paint – "

"That's right, miss," encouraged Royle. "Now lemme help you to your feet."

"Please," she whispered. When she was in a standing position Royle supported her with his left hand and with his right reached for the reins of his plunging horse. At the sight of his master approaching, the horse became more excited, throwing his head back in an effort to free itself from the greasewood. Then, before Royle could grab the leather, the stem snapped. The horse reared with a shrill whinny of triumph, turned and galloped off in a blind frenzy of fear. Royle cursed briefly and expertly, then turned to the girl.

"'Fraid we'll have to try and make it on foot, miss. Hang on to me if you want, an' I'll do my best to help you along."

"Thank you," she muttered. "Everything's going round and round." To support herself she put her arm around his neck while he clasped her waist. Idiotically he could not help thinking that in any other circumstance it would have been a very pleasant experience.

They began stumbling forward in the direction the horse had taken. The fire was closer now. Sometimes the wind carried a shower of sparks past them, sometimes the smoke was so thick that both were doubled up coughing. As they fled it seemed as if the whole of nature were fleeing with them. Rabbits bounded past in a series of agonised leaps. Lizards scuttled across patches of dried earth and a squealing wild boar went blundering past. Looking up, Royle saw a small, flaming branch carried on the wind land in front of them on a clump of crucifix thorn. The bush was so dry it exploded into flame with a crackling roar.

Royle had to drag the girl to one side to avoid it, and he knew they were now in the danger zone. At any moment the vegetation around them could blossom into a sea of fire. As he shouted encouragement to the girl, the fierce heat beat on his back and he knew that unless some miracle happened it would only be a question of minutes before they would be overtaken by the wall of flame.

He made the mistake of looking back. Serpents of flame were streaking ahead of the main line of fire, moving like hungry tongues amongst the tinder-dry vegetation. The girl was definitely holding him back. After the blow on the head she could not manage anything better than a shambling walk. He paused, lifted her into his arms as though she were a child and continued forward at a half run.

"Keep going, stranger," she muttered. "If you can keep going a bit longer we've got a chance."

By now the smoke was so thick about them that Royle's only clue to his direction was to keep the fire behind them. Twice he missed his footing and fell sprawling. The pain of his falls only sharpened his determination to carry on. He was reeling forward like a man half asleep. He was almost thankful for the sharp agony in his shoulder where he had cut it against a rock. It was a spur which would prevent him from falling into a stupor caused by the smoke.

"Just a little further," muttered the girl as though in a delirium. "A little further and we have a chance."

"What chance?" demanded Royle savagely as a small tree behind them flashed into flames and a swarm of sparks descended on Royle, burning neat holes in his shirt and pitting his back with burns.

"The river, the river," mumbled the girl. "I was

heading for the river when Paint stumbled."

Royle looked around him wildly. They were
lunging through a lurid hell of smoke and sparks. The air
was so hot it scorched his nostrils and throat with every
breath. He had lost all sense of direction and all sense of
time. It seemed an eternity since he had first smelled the
smoke and he felt half his lifetime had been spent carrying
the limp form of the girl.

Suddenly he was surrounded by trees, trees which
were blossoming with fearful blooms as fiery fragments
rained down upon them. A blazing branch suddenly
crashed in front of Royle, presenting him with a barrier of
fire. He knew that unless he went through it he was
trapped. Breathing in a lungful of acrid air, he charged the
blaze. He emerged with smouldering clothes, singed hair
and hands burned badly enough to give him a foretaste of
the hell that was bound to come.

He was aware of the ground sloping beneath his
feet. He struggled on, crashing from tree to tree, and at the
back of his mind was gratitude that the girl had fainted in
his arms.

Suddenly he slipped down a bank, and then he was
waist deep in spiky rushes like strips of brown parchment.
This must be the river the girl had muttered about. It
seemed dried up, but perhaps there was still water in the
middle of its course. He floundered on through the dead
vegetation, but even as he did so there was a terrifying
whoosh as it flash-ignited. Unable to see far ahead
because of the smoke, Royle staggered on.

Then there were no more rushes – just a narrow
strip of black mud and a sluggishly moving expanse of
water, perhaps fifty feet across. It was no time for
ceremony. Royle hurled the girl as far as he could into the
stream and blundered in after her. He found himself in
water that just came above his gunbelt, and managed to
catch hold of the girl's hair before she went under for a

second time. Then, placing his hands under her armpits, he pulled her to the centre of the stream. Here he knelt down on the bed of the river, so that only his head was visible above the surface. The shock of the water had revived the girl and she held on to his shoulder while he supported her, her black hair streaming with the current.

For a while neither spoke, savouring the coolness of the water which soothed their burns and quenched their thirst. The rushes were now ablaze and from them clouds of burning material were blown across the river, setting the rushes on the opposite side alight. A rain of sparks was hissing on the surface of the water and out of the corner of his eye Royle saw the head of a snake glide past them.

"To think of what would have happened if you had not come along," said the girl with a sudden shudder.

"Only happy to be of service, miss," Royle said. "By the way, I'm Lee Royle. I guess we didn't have time to get properly introduced."

The girl smiled for the first time and despite her smoke-grimed face and bedraggled appearance, Royle saw that it was a face of great beauty. "I'm pleased to make your acquaintance, Mister Royle. I am Ella Quinn."

CHAPTER 6

The sinking sun appeared like an enormous orange disc through the smoke haze hanging over the plain. Its dying light threw long shadows from the group of men who stood on the slope of a small hill. On the summit of the hill was a blackened skeleton of a tree, silhouetted against the livid sky like a hand twisted in agony. In the background a cowboy stood holding the reins of a number of horses. As the restless animals shifted their hooves, clouds of grey grass ash rose in the air. Here and there the embers of thorn bushes glowed briefly in the light evening breeze.

The fire had come, fed itself on a carpet of dry vegetation and rushed on, leaving a wasteland of ash and charred sagebrush. In front of the men stood a small slack man. His arms dangled limply and his narrow, ferret-face kept twisting with emotion. It was Eddy, the morose drinker of the Good Luck Saloon. Directly in front of him stood Pete Montana, dressed in his usual black.

"Have you got anythin' to say for yourself, Eddy?" he asked.

Eddy looked feverishly from one stern face to the other, but said nothing.

"You caught him red-handed?" continued Montana, turning to Sam Cash.

"Sure did, Pete," said Sam Cash. "I found him ridin' along settin' fires going as merry as you please. If you go over to his cayuse there you'll see he is carryin' a good supply of mineral oil to help things along."

"I guess he was hopin' that the wind would carry the fire right up the valley," said one of the Circle-Star riders in the background. "Durn good thing the wind dropped when it did, or it might have reached the ranch house by now."

"I guess we'd better take him back to Boss Quinn," said another rider. "I wouldn't like to be in his shoes, though. I guess the old man must be plumb crazy with his daughter missin'."

"I give the orders here," snapped Montana. "These goddamned ranchers and smallholders need a lesson, and I'm gonna give 'em one. Got a lariat, Sam?"

At last Eddy found words. "You ain't gonna –" he began and then his voice broke into a sob. "Please, boys, I gotta wife."

"So what?" Pete Montana said roughly. "Boss Quinn had a daughter till you came along settin' fire to the range."

Eddy dropped to his knees in the ash. Hysterically he begged the silent men to save him. "Let me go an' I'll tell you somethin'," he said. "I know of a plan. Yeah, yeah, a very important plan. A plan to blow up your dam. I'll tell you all about it. I'll tell you who's gonna do it. But don't, don't – "

Some of the Circle-Star men shuffled uncomfortably, embarrassed by what they saw in front of them.

"Let's get it over, boys," Pete said. "Where's your lariat, Sam?"

Sam Cash looked coolly at Pete Montana. "Use your lariat, *compadre*," he said. "It was your idea, so you do it. I may be a lot of things, but I ain't a hangman."

Montana turned to him with smouldering eyes. He seemed to have forgotten Eddy, who was now writhing full length. He ran his forefinger over his short trim moustache, then he said: "You're getting kind of sassy, Sam. You seem to forget that I'm Boss Quinn's number one man and you're just a hired gun. You ain't trying to start somethin', are you?"

"Aw, think what you like," Cash retorted. "I'm not stoppin' you from hangin' him, I'm just saying don't use my lariat. There's killin' and killin', I reckon."

"Well, who would have thought the great Sam Cash gets yeller when it comes to a hangin'?" said Pete Montana. There was a silence, broken only by the moaning of Eddy. Then Sam Cash walked over to his horse and climbed into the saddle, where he sat watching the proceedings with an expressionless face.

"All right," said Montana, "Throw your lariat over that branch up there, Curtis."

A man took a coiled rope from his saddle, expertly tested the slipknot at the end and then went up the hill where he threw it over a branch.

"Okay," said Montana. "You know what to do." He advanced on Eddy who began to scream. Pathetically he tried to shake them off but within a minute his arms were behind his back and his wrists tied together. A horse was led forward and he was raised to the saddle. The noose of the lariat was placed round his neck and he looked with wide-eyed terror straight at the sun which was now partly below the horizon. Pete Montana seized the reins of the horse.

"Anything you want to say?" he demanded.

There was no answer.

"Get up," cried Montana to the horse, and tugged on the rein. The horse sprang forward and Eddy was left dangling in the air. His body jerked grotesquely as the cruel pressure of the rope cut off the air from his lungs.

A few minutes later the party of Circle-Star men rode off. The body of Eddy swung free below the branch of the tree. It spun slowly from west to north, to east, to south and on its shirt was pinned a note which read: "Fire-raisers beware."

* * *

"Have another whisky, son," said Boss Quinn. "You sure look as though you need it." The owner of the Circle-Star was sitting in the living-room of his ranch house. Royle, pale-faced and singed, was sitting opposite him, a bandage on his left wrist where he had been particularly badly scorched. As Quinn passed over the bottle he said: "I still can't quite believe it's true, son. I really thought I'd lost her. I knew she was out ridin' in the place where the fire started, and when it came up to the walls of The Plateau an' she hadn't turned up I didn't think there could be a chance. And there wouldn't have been if you hadn't come along when you did. I had my outfit searchin' everywhere. An' then, I saw the two of you coming up the valley. I'll never forget that as long as I live."

"Neither will I," smiled Royle bleakly. "I thought our number was up until we got to the river. Then it was just a question of wadin' upstream. Of course sometimes we had to lie right low in the water when the flames blew across. But what's left of the old Snowy sure saved us. How's Ella now?"

"Sleeping like a baby," said Boss Quinn. "Now look, Royle. Without makin' any speeches you know I'm very grateful. There would be a pretty good job here on the Circle-Star if you wanted it. I know somethin' about you already. One of my men, Sam Cash, was tellin' me about you. I could use you in these troubled times."

"Thanks for your offer, Mister Quinn," said Royle. "But I ain't really interested. I only came to Silver Bend to help my brother dig a well."

Quinn said bitterly: "I guess you see yourself on the other side."

"Not at all. I ain't on anybody's side. I was once and I learned my lesson the hard way. Now I ride alone and I like it that way. Whole trouble is everybody thinks they're right. You reckon you're entitled to put up a dam–it's your land–but I guess the small ranchers an' settlers feel equally entitled to get sore when they see their creeks runnin' dry. Personally, the only thing that makes me sore is if anybody tries to push me around. Maybe some of your guys are a mite inclined to push. We had a visit the other day from your foreman."

Boss Quinn sighed and lit himself one of his long cigars. "Yeah, I know," he said. "But look at it from my point of view. People are tryin' to needle me. We found a guy called Muldoon shooting down my cattle. Today you saw what happened. They set my range alight. Both times we got the guy who did it, an' they won't do it no more."

"It won't finish at that," mused Royle. "The only thing'll stop it is rain."

"Maybe not even that. Once men start hatin' I guess the habit sticks."

"Well, I'd like to turn in, if you don't mind. I still feel kinda shook up."

"Sure thing, son. Tomorrow I'll get you taken over to your brother's place. For a sky pilot he's not a bad guy, your brother. He's the only one of them as had the guts to ride out. I wish he wouldn't preach agin me, though. It's that sorta thing that triggers off things like what happened today. The trouble is," said the ranch owner, a weary look crossing his face,, "when things like this happen, it's pretty hard to keep my boys from gettin' rough."

"I'll bet it is," said Royle.

After a heavy, dreamless sleep of exhaustion Royle woke feeling a new man. True, his body was tender where it had been scorched but the very fact that he was alive seemed to lighten his step. It was arranged that after breakfast Ella would take him in a buggy to his brother's home.

"Maybe you'd like to see our famous dam," said Ella, as they settled themselves and she flicked the whip over the back of the bay gelding.

"Sure would, Miss Quinn," Royle said, his pulse beating a little faster as he looked at the girl beside him. Dressed demurely in pale grey and with a large hat, which he figured had come from the East, she presented a very different picture from the girl he had saved yesterday. The buggy left the Circle-Star buildings and rattled along a short track across the valley floor. Royle saw a silver shimmer of what appeared to be a large body of water. In the distance herds of black cattle were standing knee-deep along its edge drinking, while yelling cowboys brought more lowing herds across the valley and drove away those who had drunk their fill.

Closer at hand Royle saw the dam. He had not realised that it would be such a huge affair. It was constructed of tree trunks and timber, with earthwork thrown up against it except in the centre where it was a complete wall of wood with water spurting between its cracks.

Cascades leapt from the sluices and foamed angrily at the foot of the dam. It was these sluices which supplied the water to the river and which in turn fed the creeks on the plain beyond.

"I'm glad your father keeps them sluices open," Royle said, "otherwise we might not have escaped yesterday."

"Once the water drops below a certain level the river will start to dry up completely," said Ella sombrely. "It's never been as low as this in the memory of the Indians. The water that comes down from Old Snowy and feeds the river in the is getting less and less, and if it doesn't rain soon I just don't know what'll happen."

"Maybe the rainmaker will be able to do the trick," laughed Royle. "If he can make rain like he can talk, I guess we might be in for a flood."

Ella turned the head of the horse and he followed the trail south, parallel with the river. Here it was only a trickle compared with what it had been, and on each side of it were stretches of black mud. The surface of these had become rock-hard with the intense heat of the sun, then cracked into a vast mosaic.

As Royle surveyed the landscape he realised how strategically the dam had been placed. It could be raked by rifle-fire from the fortified Circle-Star ranch buildings in the event of attack.

After an hour they passed out of the valley and before them lay the thousands of acres of rangeland which had been devastated by the fire. A haze still hung over it.

"I'll have to go round this," said Ella. "In places the ground will still be hot. I hope you're not in a hurry."

Royle was in no hurry at all. As Ella talked and laughed he realised that life could be more pleasant than he had thought. At last, early in the afternoon, the buggy halted at the gate of Ethan Royle's place.

"It was mighty kind of you to bring me all this way, Miss Ella," said Royle.

"It was mighty kind of you to save my life, Mister Royle," she replied with a smile.

"I was thinkin' it would be a pity if we didn't see each other again," said Royle boldly.

"I'm glad you said that, Mister Royle. I was thinking the same thing."

They sat for a moment in silence. The horse flicked its ears impatiently as flies tormented it.

"Sometimes," said Ella, "I go for a ride in Skull Canyon. The scenery is beautiful there. Nature has carved it out of The Plateau, and there's caves in the walls where the Indians used to live long before us palefaces came."

"That's mighty interesting," said Royle. "I'd sure 'preciate seein' such a place. Mayhap you'd like to show it to me?"

"I'd be very happy to."

"I hope – uh – your Pa wouldn't mind you ridin'

out with a stranger."

"He might be angry – if he knew," laughed Ella. "He's very strict in some ways, though he lets me have my freedom in others. He knows I'm too much like him to be chained up, so I can go riding as I please and he doesn't worry because he knows I'm a real fine shot with a rifle."

"I'll remember that," laughed Royle.

"I'll see you then, at noon on Sunday at Skull Canyon," smiled Ella.

"You sure will."

Then Royle, feeling slightly strange in the clothes he had borrowed at the Circle-Star from Sam Cash, walked into the house.

"Lee, where have you been?" demanded Linda. "I've been so worried about you, but by the look of you you've been on the spree. Terrible things have happened."

"Indeed, they have," said Ethan, coming through the door. "This morning they found a man from Silver Bend hanged from a tree. It's the work of those murdering Circle-Star riders."

"If it's that guy Eddy you're talkin' about I guess he deserved to be hanged," said Royle. "Eddy was a fire-raiser and he nearly finished me off." He briefly told them of his adventures but, for some reason he did not quite understand, he played down the part Ella had played.

"The trouble is that back at Silver Bend they don't just see Eddy as a fire-raiser," said Ethan. "To them he's a man who tried to burn out a nest of varmints for keepin' the water away from their land. There's all sorts of talk of teachin' the Circle-Star a lesson, an' while I don't agree with it, I can understand how they feel. Several families are ruined an' are pullin' out in their wagons. Only the Good Lord knows what will happen to them. And two Silver Bend men have died, Luke Muldoon and Eddy."

"I know," said Royle. "But like I told Boss Quinn,

I'm not on either side. Now come on, Ethan, let's get back to that well."

"But you can't work after you've been scorched like this," protested Linda.

"I can have a durn good try," laughed Royle. "I've come a long way to dig this blamed well and I know the bettin' in Silver Bend is that we'll never reach water – but just you see. A few wells in the right places and there wouldn't be any talk of a range war."

* * *

Work on the well continued. The two brothers laboured as though their lives depended upon it. Sometimes a neighbour would ride over and sit on his horse, watch a while and chew a straw, then shake his head sadly and ride away. Whenever Linda brought them water or coffee she would look into the gaping pit and say: "My, you're a long way down now. Ain't there any water yet?"

"It'll be there," said Royle doggedly. "I can feel it through that copper wire, just waitin' to come up pure an' sparklin'. See if I ain't right."

"I hope so. I pray the Lord so," said Ethan. "The creek's shrunk to a trickle now."

"It will be interestin' to see who strikes water first, us or the rainmaker," laughed Royle, his voice muffled by the depth at which he was working. "How's he makin' out?"

"I heard tell from old Abe Jackson, who has a place down the trail, that Marshal Dolan collected enough money and Nimrod's gonna go to work. Old Abe says he's building some wooden towers just outside Silver Bend in Matt Kelly's field, in fact. Old Abe says they're about twelve feet high and they've got little platforms on top, an' the rainmaker says each one's got to be in a certain position like the points of a star, otherwise it won't work properly."

"I guess the citizens will be mighty sore if it don't work," said Royle. "One way I heard of is to fire a cannon into the sky, shooting the ball into the clouds."

"There ain't no artillery around here," said Ethan. "The nearest military post is about fifty mile away, at Avalon an' even if we had some field pieces there ain't no clouds to fire at."

"Pity somebody couldn't fire at that wretched dam," said Linda. "Don't worry," said Royle. "Sooner or later they will."

* * *

It was Saturday at sunset. A whoop of joy echoed out of the shaft. "We hit it," yelled Royle. "It's seepin' through and I got my feet wet."

"The Lord be praised," cried Ethan. He fell upon his knees, bowing his head for a moment in prayer. Then he rose and climbed down the long ladder and joined his brother at the bottom of the pit which was now turning to mud in the yellow glow of the kerosene lantern.

"We'll have to go deeper yet to give it room to fill." said Royle "Then we'll rig up buckets an' a waterin' trough for the stock. We'll get that done tomorrow mornin'."

"No," Ethan said quietly. "It's the Sabbath tomorrow."

"Yes, but don't you realise we've hit water? You could be giving it to your beeves tomorrow. As it is, they have to get belly deep in mud before they get to that miserable trickle in your creek. You've lost several that way already."

"Never mind," said Ethan quietly. "It's the Lord's Day tomorrow and I shall keep it as the Lord commanded. Besides, I have to go in to Silver Bend to give the Word."

"You sure are a determined cuss," said Royle. He bent down and, cupping his hands, took a drink of water that had now formed into a small pool at his feet.

"How is it?" asked Ethan.

"Sweet," said Royle. "There ain't nothin' as sweet as water you've just found for yourself."

Next morning Ethan Royle dressed himself in his dark suit and black, broad-brimmed hat which gave him the look of a Puritan of earlier times.

"I wish you weren't going into town today, Ethan," said Linda as she brushed his frock coat. "I'm so worried after the threats of that man Montana. Why not stay at home and leave your meetings till the drought's over?"

"There's a few people, maybe not many, who depend upon me to hold a meetin' every week. I aim to hold them their meetin's until Silver Bend has a pastor of its own. Don't you worry about Montana none–the worst thing you can do to a bully is to show you're not scared of him."

"Couldn't you go in with him?" asked Linda, turning to Royle. "At least you've got a gun."

Royle looked away. "I got some business to look to," he muttered.

"The Lord is my shepherd," said Ethan. "He will look after me without the use of firearms." A minute later the buckboard was rattling down the trail that led to Silver Bend.

Leaving Linda cooking in the kitchen, Royle went and saddled his brother's spare horse, then he set off across the plain in the direction of Skull Canyon.

* * *

It was at sundown when Royle returned to the house. He saw the buckboard was pulled up by the corral but as yet Ethan had not unharnessed the horse. He swung out of the saddle and started to lead his mount to the corral. Suddenly the kitchen door flew open.

"Lee, Lee!" cried Linda in a hysterical voice. "Damn you, come here. Ethan has been shot."

65

CHAPTER 7

Royle looked down at the grey, sweat-beaded face of his brother as he lay on the bed where Linda had somehow managed to drag him.

"My God, Linda, what's happened?" he asked.

"He's been shot," she moaned. "Shot in the back. I've done what I could. The bleeding was terrible but I've put a bandage there and it seemed to stop it a bit. If only you'd gone with him – "

"How did it happen?" demanded Royle.

"I don't know. I don't know. About half an hour ago I saw the horse bringin' the buckboard back by itself and he – he was sprawled across the seat. It's all your fault, Lee."

Royle turned to her roughly. "You blamed me for a lot of things in the past, Linda, now don't you start it again. I'll ride into town and bring back the doc. Keep him warm an' if he's thirsty just wet his lips. Don't give him anythin' to drink. I'll be back soon as I can."

He cast a final glance at his brother who made a frightening sound as he fought for his breath. Outside in the purple dusk Royle leaped into the saddle and started off down the trail as fast as he could, cursing the approaching darkness which would slow him up until the moon rose.

When he returned with the doctor, after what seemed to be an eternity, he saw Linda bending over her husband. It looked as though she had not moved since he left. Doc Miller, a tall, gangling man with huge hands and ugly steel-rimmed spectacles, followed him into the room.

"Now what seems to be the matter, Mrs. Royle?" he said in a voice of surprising gentleness for one with such a rough hewn face.

"Shot," muttered Linda. "He hasn't come to since I put him here."

"Help me cut away his clothes," said the doctor.

Deftly his scissors cut through the material of Ethan's shirt. Almost tenderly he removed the dressing Linda had placed there to disclose an ugly blue-rimmed hole in the small of Ethan's back.

"Waal," murmured Doc Miller turning to them. "I guess we got a chance. That bullet missed the vital organs, otherwise he'd have been dead by now. All I gotta do is just pull it out, an' I want you to help me. Do you get sick at the sight of blood, mister?"

"Not usually," said Royle. "But I ain't never watched surgery done before."

"Just turn away it it gets too much for you. An' hold the light close 'cause I've gotta see what I'm doin'. Mrs. Royle, heat up some water, plenty of it, as we've got to keep everything as clean as we can. Now lay him out like this and be sure he can breathe as easy as possible."

When Ethan lay in the right position, with his head turned to one side, the doctor opened his bag and drew forth a case of shining instruments the very sight of which made Royle wince. From the kitchen came the clash of utensils as Linda began heating the water.

"It's always a good trick for gettin' the womenfolk out of the way," said Doc Miller. "They make darn good nurses afterwards, but at this particular time I don't like them fussin' around me. Here we go. It's better to get it over with now, than do it later on. He can't feel anythin' while he's like this."

Taking a silver instrument he began to probe the wound. Ethan moaned in his coma and the sweat began to run down Royle's face.

"He's had a mighty close call," said the doctor. "Must have been shot from quite a long range. If it'd been

67

nearer he'd have been dead now, if my experience of gunshot wounds is anything to go by. An' believe me, mister, since I've been in this territory I've had plenty of experience of that."

He withdrew the instrument which had now turned red and which caused Royle to look away suddenly. There was a tinkle of instruments and out of the corner of his eye Royle saw the doctor holding a pair of slender forceps.

"Colt's disease is the biggest epidemic we get out this way," the doctor continued as he worked. "Apart from that the West is a healthy place."

Suddenly there was the sound of a small heavy object being dropped into a tin basin.

"There it is," said the doctor in triumph. "Now the worst's over. What we've got to do is clean up this wound, put a dressing on it and I'll give him something to take to stop fever."

With morbid curiosity Royle looked into the bowl. There lay a blood-streaked rifle bullet. "Do you know how it happened?" asked the doctor, as he made Ethan comfortable.

"No idea," said Royle. "Linda – his wife – said the horse brought the buggy back with him sprawled on it. He must have been shot somewhere down the trail. I'm sure gonna find the coyote who did it."

The doctor rose to his full shambling height.

"I was going down Main Street this afternoon and I heard him preachin'," he said. "He was doin' pretty well. Had quite a crowd. He was sayin' it was wrong to stand in the way of God's works, that when God meant man to have something he meant everybody, and not just those who were able to throw dams across rivers."

"That sure explains it then," said Royle. "Doc, I'd be much obliged if you wouldn't tell anybody in Silver Bend about this. I don't want anybody to know my brother's been hurt."

"Okay, mister, if you want it that way," said the doctor, packing up his instruments. "'Tain't none of my business. Come into town tomorrow and I'll give you some more medicines for him."

Next day in Silver Bend notices in scrawling handwriting were found tacked to the clapboard walls of several buildings on Main Street. They said, "At noon next Wednesday Brother Ethan Royle will address a meeting on the subject of God's Gift of Water."

The following afternoon Ethan's temperature dropped nearer to normal and his eyes fluttered open. For some moments he looked with a bewildered expression at the face of his wife and slowly his gaze shifted to Royle. "It hurts pretty badly," he muttered.

"Doc said it would for a while," Royle said. "When it's healed up you'll be right as rain. The thing is not to worry about anythin'. Just lie here and get well. Got any notion as to who did it?"

Ethan rolled his head wearily.

"I saw Pete Montana at the edge of the crowd when I was giving my meetin'," he said. "He looked kind of mad at some of the things I felt I had to say. When I was comin' back on the buckboard I had an idea he was followin' me. I looked back once and saw him in the distance. Then when I was right out of town I was hit. At first it didn't seem so bad. I whipped up the horse and managed to look round. But nobody was following me. It must have been a long shot, a rifle."

"So Pete Montana wouldn't know how bad you were hit," mused Royle.

"I didn't pass out for some minutes I guess, but I began to get sick and it began to feel like a hot poker twisting into me."

"Never mind now," said Royle. "You're safe an' you're gonna be all right."

He left the husband and wife together. He walked

out to the barn and carefully closed the door behind him so Linda wouldn't see what he was about to do. Somewhere a shutter occasionally flapped in the dry, drought wind. Royle stood in a half crouch and the next time the shutter banged his hand snaked down to the butt of the Frontier in its low-slung holster. He jerked the gun out and swung it up until it was level with his eye.

He tried this several times, moving each time the distant shutter gave him his cue.

"Guess it was true what Montana said," he muttered. "The aim is somethin' you're born with, you can't lose that. But the draw only comes with practice and I guess I've got slow." For the rest of the afternoon, in the hot, gloomy barn, Royle practised drawing his pistol, cursing softly at what he considered to be his clumsiness.

* * *

Jonathan Q. Nimrod surveyed his pyramid-shaped towers with satisfaction. Behind him stood Marshal Dolan and a group of Silver Bend's leading citizens.

"Well, there it is, boys," said the rainmaker, turning to them. "I'm all set to go. Now, you just hand me over that money, Marshal, an' pretty soon there'll be a downpour like you've never seen in years."

"How soon will that be, Mister Nimrod?" asked the marshal. "Do you figure on bringin' the rain down today?"

"It won't be today, gentlemen," said Jonathan Q. Nimrod. "The conditions ain't right."

"Why ain't they?" demanded Isaiah Jenkins, the local storekeeper.

The rainmaker gave him a haughty look. "If I was not a gentleman," he said ponderously, "I would call that a damn fool question, but seein' you live a mighty long distance from the centres of culture and refinement and education, I will make allowances for your goshdarned ignorance. To any man with a smattering of scientific intellect the answer would be amazingly clear. But as you've not got these advantages, I will explain – there's a wind blowing!"

"Well – uh – what's the wind got to do with the rain coming down, Mister Nimrod?" asked Marshal Dolan.

"Everything, my dear Marshal," boomed Nimrod. "While I cannot expect you to understand the intricacies of my scientific art I shall attempt to illuminate the fog that seems to abound in your cerebral cavity. You see these here towers, Marshal? On each one of these towers I put a tub and in each tub there is a certain chemical. When I set them chemicals on fire the smoke rises into the air. Now the rain that I'm going to bring down is floating very high up, an' as my chemical smoke rises it gradually mixes until, at the right height, it all blends together to form an amorphous elixir which men of science have sought to discover for many centuries. Therefore, if there is a high wind blowing, my columns of smoke will not rise straight into the air and mingle at the right height. As you know, they will be swept away and lost."

"Dang me, that's a real problem," said Jenkins. "Sometimes the wind keeps blowing in these parts for weeks."

"Mebbe for another thousand bucks he could stop the wind," drawled an unbeliever at the edge of the group.

"Now, gentlemen," said the rainmaker leading the way towards the marshal's office, "as soon as the wind drops I shall light my chemicals and the glorious heavenly dew will come pattering down ... I must be careful not to overdo it otherwise you might get a fall of snow."

At his office door Marshal Dolan looked embarrassed.

"There's one thing I've got to say, Mister Nimrod," he faltered, fiddling with his star of office. "Some of the

71

boys figger it ain't right to pay you the money – uh – until the rain starts to fall, if you see what I mean – "

There was a silence. Nimrod slowly looked from face to face and then drawing up to his full towering height he said, "Gentlemen, an' I only use that term as a mere formality, in twenty years of successful rainmaking I have never heard of such a preposterous insult. I can only believe that you have no faith in me – or maybe you are so mean you plan to hold on to the money when the drought's broke. I guess I can understand it, seein' as you come from such an ignorant, pinch-gutted, one-hoss town.

"In good faith I have built my towers, have mixed my precious chemicals. As soon as the wind drops I am ready to save you from disaster. But now you tell me you do not wish to shell out, which can only mean that in your secret heart of hearts you believe I am some mountebank, some wandering salesman of quack cures. Let me tell you, citizens of Silver Bend, you are not dealin' with some downtrodden purveyor of snake oil medicaments – No siree, you're dealin' with Jonathan Q. Nimrod and if you come to my wagon I'll show you papers which give me degrees and titles from the most famous European universities, Heidelberg, Padua and Paris.

"And now I say to you, gentlemen, keep your miserable money. Clasp it tight to your bosoms. I hope when you run out of drinkin' water, it'll be a comfort. I'll go on to the next community that can use my services, and will suitably show gratitude to someone who has come to help them in their hour of need, who will recognise an .eminent man of science when they see one – not haggle over a few, lousy, goddam dollars. I bid you good day," and turning on his heel he walked purposefully in the direction of his yellow-painted wagon.

"Goshdarn it," said Marshal Dolan. "That's done it. I was scared he'd act that way if I told him. What're we going to do now? I guess the fellows that chipped in will be pretty mad when they see him leavin' town."

"Better call him back and give him the money," said Jenkins. "After all, it ain't our money, Marshal."

"Guess you're right," said Dolan, unhappily. "Just to make sure, I'll get my deputy to keep an eye on his wagon so he don't skip until the rains come."

"Okay, Marshal," said Jenkins. "I'll go over and ask him to come back to your office."

After a lot of pleading Jonathan Q. Nimrod allowed himself to be coaxed into taking the money in advance for his services.

Wednesday dawned clear and breathless. For a brief period before the sun hoisted itself into the sky there was a pleasant coolness, but this was soon to go. The landscape of the plains and the distant plateau, which for a brief period appeared diamond-clear and closer to the town than it really was, began to shimmer in the overheated air. But the great thing about this Wednesday was the drought wind had dropped. Men wet their fingers to test it and their spittle dropped plumbline straight to the ground.

For once there was an air of excitement in Silver Bend. Citizens began to flock round the yellow wagon of the rainmaker and a ragged cheer went up as that gentleman drove in the direction of his towers. Though he beamed confidently at this encouragement, the rainmaker was secretly apprehensive. He had been acutely aware of a certain young man with a stubborn expression, Marshal Dolan's deputy, who had been following him like a disagreeable shadow for the past two days.

At the site of the towers Jonathan Q. Nimrod began unloading some sacks which had strange signs stencilled on them. Taking these he poured the contents into the tubs which he had mounted on small platforms on top of the towers. When his tubs were filled he sprinkled gunpowder on the top as the agent to set the chemicals burning. There

73

was another cheer from the assembled crowd when he put a match to the first tub and the powder burst into yellow flame. Soon all the chemicals had been ignited and columns of smoke began to ascend.

"How long will it take now, Mister Nimrod?" asked Marshal Dolan.

"These will have to burn all day," replied the rainmaker. "I guess the rain will start coining down some time tonight."

"Hear that, folks," cried the marshal. "We're in for a wet night." There was laughter and more cheers and the rainmaker went from tower to tower checking that the contents of the tubs were smouldering in a correct fashion. For most of the morning the crowd watched, gazing up at the pillars of smoke which rose so straight they almost appeared to be solid. Whatever the ingredients were in Jonathan Q. Nimrod's tubs at least they gave forth a satisfactory black smoke and already the citizens of Silver Bend felt they were getting their money's worth.

The rainmaker's performance was equally good. Sometimes he would pore over a sheet of calculations, hastily scribbling out equations, then add some powder to one tub or another.

At noon some of the crowd began to drift off. The word had spread that the preacher had come in for his special meeting. In Main Street they saw him take up his usual position, his dark hat was pulled down over his eyes to shade them from the glare of the midday sun, but despite the heat his black frock coat was neatly buttoned as he stood with hands clasped together ready to preach.

"Come on, brethren," he cried. "Come close round my wagon. There's some mighty important things I've got to say."

A small crowd clustered round while others watched from the shade of the veranda. Several men casually sauntered out of the Silver Lode Saloon and

74

stood on the outskirts of the crowd. The assembled citizens were quick to notice that one of them was Pete Montana, The preacher stood for a moment looking around him as though looking for inspiration.

"Come on, padre," encouraged a voice. "Give us the Good Word an' plenty of hellfire."

The preacher cleared his throat. "Friends," he said, "I want you to look at that," and he pointed to where the columns of the rainmaker's smoke towered skywards above the buildings of Silver Bend. "A lot of you folk here think that smoke is gonna turn into rain. Well, I ain't going to say it ain't, but it seems to me it's a mighty hard way of goin' about gettin' what you need. I would say, friends, that it ain't necessary. Why do I say that? I'll tell you for why. Not far from here is all the water we need comin' down the Snowy River. There it is, folks, a whole lake of it glitterin' in the sun. Thousands an' thousands of gallons of cool water, that we could be using for our stock – if it weren't for the fact that a man has placed himself above the Lord and damned up the Lord's river –" There was a stunned silence and the eyes of the onlookers swivelled from the tall figure of the preacher to the face of Pete Montana. He took a pace forward and then said: "I warned you against preachin' against Boss King, Royle. I thought I'd taught you a lesson. This time I'm gonna make sure."

Imperceptibly the crowd moved back so there was a clear space round the two actors in the drama. With his face in the shadow of his low-tilted hat the preacher looked down at the gunman. With a thin sadistic smile on his face, Montana put his left hand on his right pistol butt and his right hand on the left, ready for his famous cross-draw.

"I'm gonna give you five seconds to ask my pardon then get out of town, never to come back," he drawled. "One – two –"

In his nervousness the preacher had been fumbling with the buttons of his frock coat. Suddenly it fell back and there was a gasp of amazement as the onlookers saw the Colt Frontier strapped to his leg.

"It ain't him, it's his brother," yelled someone. The next second Pete Montana went for his gun and so did Lee Royle.

When the shooting was discussed at leisure, it was agreed that Pete Montana got his bullet away first. Although he carried two guns, he only used one weapon at a time, like most two-gun men, changing weapons when the first had emptied its cylinder.

Royle had taken up his position with his back to the sun. It was thought afterwards that this was what caused Montana to miss. Royle, on the other hand, swung his pistol up to eye level and fired with cool deliberation. The Frontier slug caught the Circle-Star foreman in the chest. He coughed and then sprawled forward in the dust. For a moment there was a stunned silence. Then the doors of the Silver Lode swung open and about a dozen Circle-Star riders ran out.

"My Gawd, Montana's been shot," yelled one.

After that, confusion broke out. The crowd melted as the Circle-Star men began firing at Royle. He jumped down from the buckboard and ran down the street in the direction of the Good Luck Saloon. A fusillade of lead whined after him. Somewhere there was the tinkle of breaking glass as a stray bullet smashed a window.

Before Royle reached the batwing doors of the Good Luck he flattened himself against its wall, threw up his gun and sent a couple of shots into the line of Circle-Star men who had spread across the street. As he fired the crack of a rifle rang sharply in his ear. He turned and saw Jason Shepherd on one knee beside him, smoke streaming from the muzzle of his Winchester.

"Damn fine shootin', Royle," he gasped. "If

they're gonna get you, they'll get me as well. There's several of the boys here that'll put up a fight with you. Better get back into the saloon. We'll be buzzard meat if we stay out here."

Firing rapidly, the two men edged back along the wall and then dived through the doors into the saloon.

"What's goin' on?" quavered the barkeeper.

"You'll find out soon enough," said Jason Shepherd. He ran over to one of the windows, smashed it with the butt of the Winchester and poked the barrel out. Several members of the Silver Bend Cattlemen's Protection Association seemed to have materialised. Jason turned to them.

"This is where I guess we've gotta make a stand, boys," he growled. "There's enough Circle-Star men in town to surround this place. If anyone wants to leave he's still got a chance to get out of the back door, but he'd better go fast."

Nobody moved and Royle could see from the expressions on their faces that after the weeks of inaction they welcomed what was about to happen. Here at last was a chance to hit at the enemy.

"Some of you guys had better go to the top windows," said Royle. "Make sure the back's covered. We'll most like have to stand siege here."

By this time the firing had died down and, as Royle took a quick glance down the street, it seemed strangely deserted.

"They're probably surrounding us now," said Jason.

"Bill, you and Frankie push the piano across the doorway."

"Don't you damn well dare," protested the bartender, "That piano cost a hell of a lot of dollars."

Somewhere a gun barked, a bullet hummed through the doorway and crashed into the mirror behind the bar.

"There's your answer, Charlie," Jason snapped. Suddenly one of the men at the upstairs windows yelled out, "Someone coming down the street with a flag of truce. Looks like Curtis."

Cautiously Royle and Jason Shepherd looked through the windows. A Circle-Star rider was walking towards them down the middle of the street, a dirty white handkerchief tied to a stick which he kept waving furiously.

"Don't shoot, fellas," he yelled. "I got a message for you."

"Let's have it then," said Jason Shepherd.

"Let me put down this durned stick," Curtis begged. "I feel a darn fool walking around wavin' this thing."

"Go ahead," said Jason. "We won't fire unless you pull a gun on us. What have you got to say?"

"It's just this. You hand over Royle to us and we won't bother you no more."

"You've got to be makin' a joke," said Jason Shepherd. "He shot your man down in fair fight and there was no call for you lot to come pullin' your guns on him. He stays here and we stay with him."

"If that's the way you want it, that's how it'll be then," said Curtis. "You're durned fools. You're surrounded by Circle-Star boys and there'll be more coming down from the ranch to help, but maybe that's a good thing. You goddam settlers are ready for a lesson."

"Git goin'," ordered Jason Shepherd. "It's about time we had a showdown."

Curtis shrugged, picked up his stick with the handkerchief on it and ran back down the road. Seconds later a Circle-Star gunman, who had climbed on to the flat roof of the general store opposite, began firing at the windows of the Good Luck Saloon.

78

The people who were still watching Jonathan Q. Nimrod's pillars of smoke heard the shooting and removed themselves within seconds. The rainmaker was left like some early prophet in front of his fires of sacrifice and, like an early prophet, he looked heavenwards with an expression of intense gratitude on his face. Then he slipped round to the livery stable and threw a saddle over a horse which his agent had thoughtfully left for him.

Within minutes he was galloping down the trail which led from Silver Bend. Only after an hour of hard riding did he pull up his lathered mount. Looking back at the fingers of smoke on the horizon he heaved a deep sigh of satisfaction. Too bad he'd had to leave the wagon behind, but it only owed him a hundred dollars and a tin of yellow paint. He flicked his reins and set off again along the trail, his saddlebags jingling merrily.

CHAPTER 8

Ford Vance lay on the roof of the store opposite the Good Luck Saloon. The sun beat on his back, staining his shirt black with sweat. Its heat almost made him drowse as he rested his cheek on the stock of his rifle. In the street below the men of the Circle-Star crouched behind corners and walls, water butts and wagons. They had taken up every vantage point from where they could pump streams of bullets through the shattered windows of the Good Luck Saloon, or shoot down anyone who tried to make a run for it. Yet, if a stranger had looked down Main Street he would have thought the town deserted, except for the sound of gunfire and the gunsmoke which drifted between the buildings.

The besieged in the saloon fired back sporadically. Relying on the cartridges in their ammunition belts, they were reluctant to waste bullets and fired only at gun flashes to warn the Circle-Star men not to attempt a rush.

Ford changed his position slightly, swinging his foresight level at an upstairs window on the other side of the wide street. He had been in the Good Luck Saloon several times and knew this particular room was sometimes used for card games. He had once lost his month's pay at a game of faro there. Now it gave him a certain satisfaction to send a slug crashing through the glass.

The acrid smell of his burnt powder tingled pleasantly in his nostrils. It brought back a memory of when he was a kid and his Pa had presented him with a squirrel gun and shown him how to weigh the charge. He had been so proud as he had gone off into the woods with that gun. He felt he could take on any gunman in the State.

And now here he was, a few years later, swapping lead with a murdering bunch of smallholders, among whom was a man with a past reputation of a top gun. He felt that this baptism of flying bullets had at last proved his manhood.

The minutes crawled by. Once Ford thought he saw a sign of movement at the window and put another bullet through it. There was an instant reply and a .45 slug struck the parapet near him, then whined into the vastness of the sky. He ducked his head. The thought that if that bullet had been a few more inches to the left it would have probably drilled his skull brought him up with a jolt. So far it had seemed slightly unreal, like a game played as a kid. He wriggled along the roof to the parapet at the opposite end to take up a new and safer position. He could still cover the front door of the saloon, but he knew it was unlikely that anyone would try to break out. It was obvious that the members of the Silver Bend Cattlemen's Protection Association had piled up barricades of furniture behind the doors and windows. Apart from sniping each other there would be little action for a while. Behind the saloon the rainmaker's columns of smoke flowed straight upwards. They gave Ford inspiration.

"Doggone!" he exclaimed to himself. "That's what we oughta do – burn 'em out!"

There was a sharp fusillade of shots from behind the Good Luck Saloon followed by a yell. Ford could not make up his mind as to whether somebody had been hit or whether it was a cry of defiance.

Looking down he saw Curtis sprawled full length behind a bale of hay. He seemed to be watching a particular window over the sights of his pistol. Ford knew that that pistol was a break-open Smith & Wesson, a gun that Curtis had particularly fancied. He remembered how they had argued about it in the bunkhouse. Curtis had claimed it was a better gun than the Peacemaker because

81

of its ejection system.

"Hey, Curtis," yelled Ford boyishly, "let's see what you can do with that durned old cannon of yours."

As if in reply Curtis fired three times in rapid succession. Two bullets plunked into the clapboard of the saloon while a third hummed through an already shattered window. From inside the bar came the sound of broken glass and fluent cursing.

"I sure hate to think of all that whisky going to waste," Curtis yelled up to Ford. "It's probably all those poor critturs have to drink. I guess if we wait long enough they'll drink 'emselves to death."

Not to be left out of the warfare, Ford blazed away in the direction of the Good Luck sign. It amused him to put a couple of bullet holes in the centre of the ornate gilt Os in the 'good', the lettering being the only elegant thing about the square building. As he was reloading he heard a sound behind him. For a second he froze with some thought of an enemy creeping up, but it was Boss Quinn coming in a low crouch over to the roof beside him.

"How's it goin' Vance?" asked the Boss.

"Mighty fine," said Ford. "They'll never get outa there alive. They'll be perforated soon as they set foot outside."

"But I guess they may be able to hold out a while inside," said Boss Quinn.

"I think maybe we could get some of the rainmaker's chemicals an' smoke 'em out," Ford suggested eagerly.

"Not a bad notion," said Boss Quinn. "That'll teach 'em some sort of a lesson. God damn it, they shoot my cattle, they burn my range and now they've killed my best man. They've gone too far, Vance."

"It was Royle what did it," said Ford.

"Yeah, that's the hell of it. He saved my daughter from the fire and now he's shootin' my men. Damn this

82

drought. It makes everybody crazy. Anyways, I wanna get this over quickly. If it hangs on they'll get supporters riding into town from the outlyin' places. A quick, sharp lesson, that's what they need."

"That fella Royle ought to be hung for a murderin' coyote," said Ford. "He fooled Montana. Dressed up as a sky pilot, he did. Dolan shoulda gone after him right away."

"Now that's a thought," said Boss Quinn to himself. He slapped Ford on the back. "Keep fightin' boy. Got enough ammunition?"

"Guess so."

"I'll send you some up, an' some water. Keep your eyes skinned. There's about a dozen men in there and they're all pretty mean. Some of them are damn good shots."

"Don't worry about me, Boss," said Ford. "It's just like shootin' squirrels."

Boss Quinn laughed and went back across the roof. Left alone Ford began to feel sleepy again. The heat seemed to be sucking the energy from his body, and he lay in a pleasant state of laziness, occasionally pulling his trigger to let his friends know he was still in the fight. His mind flicked back to a certain young woman who he hoped would be Mrs. Vance when he had saved up enough money. He figured that after this afternoon Boss Quinn would probably be handing out some pretty hefty bonuses. He might be able to ride the fifty miles over to her Pa's place and tell him he wanted to get hitched right away. That would give them al| a bit of a surprise, especially when the word got round that he had been one of the men in the battle of Silver Bend.

With these thoughts in his mind he shifted his body into a comfortable position. There was the crash of a gun at the window on the other side of the street. The bullet caught Ford Vance full in the face and he died without a sound. It was hours later before he was found.

Down Main Street, away from the gunsmoke, Boss Quinn stumped in the Marshal's office. Dolan was sprawled in his dangerously tilted chair moodily regarding a half-empty bottle of Old Vermont. Looking through the bars of the prison door which adjoined the gloomy office was Ted Hawkins, Silver Bend's only remaining prospector and an habitual drunk. Clenching the bars with his horny hands, he looked longingly at the bottle on the marshal's table.

"Dolan, if you was a natural man, you'd give me a shot of that Vermont," he called. "I got a head that's drivin' me crazy. It's so bad I keep fancyin' I can hear shootin'."

The marshal ignored him, lost in a morass of his problems.

"Come on, Marshal," said the grizzled old man. "Ain't I one of your best customers? Don't I deserve some consideration? If you carry on like this I'll leave town and go some-wheres else and let someone else earn their pay by arrestin' me each week. I'll find me a marshal who knows how to treat a fella fair an' square after he's been celebratin'. Not that there's anything to celebrate around here."

"Marshal Dolan," said Boss Quinn, also ignoring the entreaties of Silver Bend's only prisoner. "I want you to go out an' do your duty."

The marshal looked up from his reverie sorrowfully. "An' what would you exactly say my duty was, Mister Quinn?"

"I'd say it was this, Marshal Dolan. I'd say you should walk down the street to the Good Luck Saloon and restore law and order. And at the same time I'd say you should arrest Royle on the charge of murderin' one of my men, Pete Montana."

"That's a pretty tall order, Mister Quinn. For one

thing, if you call your men off, law and order would be restored pronto. And for another thing, I don't rightly know that Royle was in the wrong. Mebbe it was a fair fight. I wasn't there. But I'll tell you this. I ain't got any hankerin' to go tradin' bullets with a guy who can use a gun like him."

"Listen, Dolan," cried Boss Quinn impatiently. "I don't want him killed. I owe him a favour. I just want you to bring him in an' chuck him in the hoosegow. We can sort it out later. But while he's in there, firin' at my boys, I can't call off. It's your duty, Marshal, and you darn well know it. Now, I'm tellin' you, get down the street an' tell Royle you're gonna take him into protective arrest."

Slowly and deliberately the marshal poured himself three fingers of Old Vermont.

"Would you like a shot yourself, Mister Quinn?" he enquired, the alcohol in his blood changing his mood to elaborate politeness. "You wouldn't? Well it don't matter none. Now what was I gonna say?"

"I don't give a cuss what you was goin' to say, Dolan. I'm tellin' you to get out an' earn your money. Go down to the Good Luck. That's an order. If you're too darned yellow to do it yourself, send your deputy."

"Now that raises a problem," Dolan mumbled reflectively. "My deputy seems to be inside the Good Luck Saloon, bein' attacked by your boys."

"Guess you'll have to do it yourself," said Boss Quinn. To emphasise his words he drew his old Texas Paterson.

"Now there ain't no call for that sort of thing, Mister Quinn," said Dolan. "You see you ain't exactly abreast of the situation. I resigned from being marshal of this town half an hour ago. Look." He pointed to his waistcoat where there was no longer a star.

"I figured I was gettin' a bit long in the tooth to be marshal, Mister Quinn. In fact I was talking to a fella

85

about going into the rainmakin' business."

With a curse Boss Quinn turned on his heel and stalked into the street.

Sam Cash holstered his Navy Colt and leaned back against the wall. With his left hand he fumbled in the breast pocket of his shirt and pulled out a small bag. He carefully sprinkled the powdered tobacco along a cigarette paper and after one quick lick rolled it skilfully into a smoke. When it was satisfactorily alight he drew his gun again and moved back into a firing position. Before he could take aim a hand fell on his shoulder. Turning, he saw the craggy features of Boss Quinn.

"Hi, Mister Quinn," he said with a grin. "Guess we're earnin' our pay at last."

"'Fraid so," said the boss of the Circle-Star. "I was talkin' to young Vance a while back an' he had a bright notion. He reckoned on gettin' some of that durned rainmaker's chemicals, puttin' 'em in a can, throwin' it into the Good Luck and smokin' the varmints out."

"The trouble would be gettin' close enough to throw it in," said Sam Cash. "In that saloon there's one of the best shots I've ever seen. Wouldn't fancy my chances against him once we're out in the open."

"Sure, sure," Boss Quinn agreed. "But look, there's an alley between the Good Luck an' the next buildin', an' from what I remember there's only one window in the wall of the saloon there. If someone could get into that alley from the back, an' scout up the side of the saloon, he could lob in a charge without any fuss."

"That somebody being me, you mean?" asked Sam Cash.

"You must have second sight," growled Boss Quinn. "At the corral is the rainmaker's wagon. Old Jack Martin is fixing up the canister for you. He's an expert on blastin'. All you have to do is light a fuse, toss it through the window an' hightail it. The place'll be filled with thick black smoke an' we'll teach those sons of bitches a lesson like they never had."

"Does that go for Lee Royle too?"

"Yep. I done what I could – tried to get him arrested. Figured I owed him a favour, but it seems Silver Bend is without a marshal. I can't do nothin' more."

"Okay," said Sam Cash with a shrug. "You pay the wages."

Half an hour later Sam Cash, body flattened to the wall, edged along the alleyway that led between the Good Luck Saloon and the Silver Bend Grain and Provision Store. From nearby came the sound of firing. Cash paid little attention to it, concentrating on the heavy canister he was carrying in both hands. From the top, like the wick from a lamp, protruded a fuse, the kind used by miners for setting off blasting charges. He paused close to the small window. Those who knew the geography of the Good Luck Saloon had told him it was unlikely to be guarded, but he thought they were saying this to encourage him rather than to impart real information. He bent down and lit the fuse of the canister.

There was a storeroom on the other side of the window and the fuse was long enough to give Cash time to retreat before the charge went off and the billowing smoke led the besieged to think their citadel was afire.

Sam Cash was about to pick up the heavy canister when his highly developed instinct for self-preservation made him glance up to see the steel-rimmed eye of a Frontier Colt regarding him coldly. Level with the Colt's barrel was a familiar face.

"Well, howdy, Royle," he said and raised his hands.

"Howdy, Sam," said Royle. "It's a funny old world. I never thought I'd meet you like this."

"Sure is, Royle," said Sam with an odd smile. "No hard feelin's."

"I'm not on anybody's side except my own. My quarrel with Pete Montana was that he shot my brother. Nothin' else."

"Well, no hard feelin's anyway," said Sam Cash, imperceptibly beginning to lower his hands. "What you aim to do? Are you gonna plug me?"

"I couldn't plug you cold, Sam," Royle said. "I'll have to give you a chance to get your spurs back."

Sam's eyes narrowed, the smile was frozen on his face. Royle recognised the killer look transforming his features and knew that any second Sam would go for his gun, in the knowledge that he wouldn't shoot until the Navy Colt was unholstered. The slightest hesitancy on his part and he could expect a bullet. He knew the logical thing to do was to squeeze his trigger before Cash went into action, yet in his mind's eye he saw again the unknown robber with the axe collapsing in the moonlight. The mental picture was interrupted by the cold voice of Sam Cash, a voice now devoid of his usual good nature.

"It's got to be, Royle," he snarled and his right hand shot down to his thigh. But before he could draw there was a flash of flame. On the ground the forgotten canister exploded, throwing Royle back from the window and slamming Sam Cash on his back halfway down the alley.

Following the blast, dense clouds of chemical smoke filled the alleyway. In the confusion and darkness Sam Cash, choking with every breath, crawled away. When he finally staggered to safety from behind the grain store his comrades gave a hoot of laughter.

"Goshdarn it, there must be a minstrel show in town," laughed Curtis.

"How about a coon song?" jeered another.

Sam Cash cursed automatically and wandered dazedly in the direction of the Silver Lode where he hoped to revive himself with some medicinal potions he knew were stocked there in abundance.

Inside the Good Luck Saloon Royle, equally black, was sluicing his face over a tin bowl of water. Fumes from the home-made smoke bomb had drifted into the bar room, but, as the device had ignited outside, most of the smoke was billowing skywards in company with the columns from the dying fires of the departed rainmaker. As he tenderly wiped his inflamed eyes, Royle knew the explosion had only postponed the showdown between himself and Sam Cash. The ultimate duel was still to come.

CHAPTER 9

There was a lull in the shooting. From his position at the window looking out on to Main Street, Lee Royle turned his head to see Jason Shepherd beside him.

"How's it goin'?" he asked.

"We're doin' all right," replied the leader of the Silver Bend Cattlemen's Protection Association. "So far the only grief is Johnny getting a flesh wound in the hip. Ain't worryin' him too much. He's up on the roof now with his Remington. I reckon if we can hold out long enough the word will get round. The other members of the Association will get together and ride in. They can take Quinn's mob from the rear. Damn good job too. This is a real war at last. Jest in passin' I'm sure glad to have a man like you on our side."

Royle rubbed the back of his hand across his red-rimmed eyes. "Well, Mister Shepherd, I wouldn't say I was exactly on your side though I'm fightin' beside you now. Fact is, I ain't on nobody's side. I'm sorta neutral, only I got mixed up in this 'cause my brother was plugged in the back by Pete Montana. Ethan would have been all for turning the other cheek, but I don't work that way. I had to get Montana an' I did just that. That's the only reason I'm in the Good Luck Saloon now."

Jason Shepherd gave him a cool look. "You ought to know by now, Royle, you've gotta be on one side or the other. Ain't any room for the guy who wants to be on his lonesome."

"Yeah, but you've gotta realise I ain't got land here. Soon as I get my well workin' I'll be movin' on. Sooner or later the drought'll have to break and it'll be all over."

"It'll never be all over. My boys'll always remember how Boss Quinn started this war. He's gotta be driven out. There ain't room for guys like him in the West no more. His name's Quinn an' he figures he is one. I tell you, Royle, he's got us out-numbered, an' he's got us bottled up in here, but pretty soon the cards will change an' he'll find out what it's like to be sieged. Put your loop round my words."

"Things are gettin' pretty quiet," Royle said. "I don't like it. I wonder what they're plotting. I think I'll mosey up onto the roof."

The mid-afternoon sun made the corrugated iron of the roof almost red-hot to the touch. Royle squirmed alongside Johnny, the man who had received the flesh wound. He was at a corner of the building, squinting down the street in the direction of the Silver Lode Saloon. Apart from a little running figure in the distance Silver Bend could have been deserted. Johnny was one of the few men in the besieged camp who had a rifle, the others having to make do with their sidearms.

"Wish we had a few long guns," Royle said. "I guess nearly all the Circle-Star fellas have."

"Yeah," agreed the young man. "I bet it was a Winchester that got me in the leg. But don't fret on it, the Colts'll do the job if they try an' rush us."

"I don't think they'll do that. My money says Boss Quinn'll go in for somethin' more crafty. Whatever it is, he'll wanna get it over quick, before reinforcements come in."

"If they do," said Johnny cynically. "If words was bullets there wouldn't be a single Circle-Star man left alive, but when the lead's flyin' I guess quite a few squatters suddenly find they've gotta hoe the cabbage patch."

Suddenly there was the sound of a shot at the rear.

"There goes Ulysses," said Johnny. "I'm sorry for

the poor crittur that gets in his sight. He's one of the best shots in the district. Wish there were a few more of his breed in Silver Bend."

"Who is he?"

"Jason Shepherd's younger brother. I guess their Ma and Pa had some pretty fancy notions about namin' them. They were called after a coupla Greek fellas, I hear tell."

Suddenly Johnny's eyes narrowed and he swivelled the rifle. Royle saw a slight movement at the corner of the hardware store opposite. Next second Johnny fired and a wraith of dust drifted up from the bullet's impact close to where the movement had been. The shot triggered off a reaction. Several bullets from different directions whined over the Good Luck Saloon's roof and the two men lay with their heads down until the firing died away. Then Johnny rolled over on his back and looked into the pitiless sky. "Goddam this war," he snarled. "I oughta be back at my place, ladlin' water out of my mud-hole for my beeves. What with Boss Quinn an' the drought, it's pretty hard for a simple man to make an honest livin' in these parts."

In the Silver Lode Saloon, at the other end of town, Boss Quinn leaned back against the bar, a whisky in his hand. Several of his men were standing around, including Sam Cash, but the shaggy-headed boss of the Circle-Star was looking directly at a tall, wide-shouldered gunman in front of him.

The eyes of this man were a pale, watery blue and when he smiled, which was on rare occasions, it could be seen that his two front teeth were crossed, giving him a strangely sinister aspect. Unlike the other Circle-Star men who were in range clothes and wore Stetsons, this snag-toothed individual wore a brown derby, a waistcoat with a watch chain across it, and a city-style coat. He might have been taken for a smart travelling salesman if it were not for the heavy holster he wore low down on his left thigh, being left-handed by nature.

He dressed in the fashion of the East, as though he wanted to make sure he could not be mistaken for a cowpuncher. In fact he was much more than that, especially now that Pete Montana was lying under a horse blanket waiting with the endless patience of the dead for the time for him to be conveyed to the small cemetery outside Silver Bend.

"Keep your cayuse movin' when you come down Main Street, Slim," Boss Quinn was saying. "Now Pete has cashed his chips you're top man an' I don't want you gettin' perforated. Just pay out the rope an' ride like hell. Don't stop to swap lead with them varmints."

"Don't you worry, Mister Quinn. A few minutes from now they won't know what's hit 'em. We'll put the score right for Pete."

There was a muttered agreement at this.

"You're dead right," said one of the men. "They set the range alight, they tried to murder us an' it sure is about time we put these goddam sons of bitches down once and for all."

"Okay, boys," Boss Quinn said. "We'll drink to that. Keep 'em pinned down with your fire while Slim comes down the street, okay?"

The men nodded, holding out their glasses while Boss Quinn filled them from a whisky bottle.

"Here's to the Circle-Star, the finest outfit west of New York," cried someone enthusiastically. They laughed and raised their glasses. Then they jingled to the door. Boss Quinn continued to lean against the counter, thoughtfully watching his men swagger.

"Hey, Sam," he called.

Sam Cash turned and walked back to him.

"Yeah, what is it, Boss?"

"You know that guy Lee Royle well?"

"Not all that well," replied Sam with a shrug. "We rode the trail into Silver Bend together."

"What sort of a guy is he?"

"I don't rightly know. There's somethin' about him I can't figure exactly. It's as though part of the time he's not one hundred per cent there ... as though part of him was away some place else. But I'll tell you one thing for free, he's the only guy that scares me with a gun round here."

"A durned shame he's teamed up with the squatters," said Boss Quinn.

"Aw, he ain't on anybody's side," Sam Cash said. "Maybe not even his own,"

"I guess he's on the other side right at this moment," remarked Boss Quinn grimly.

"If I thought –" began Sam Cash, but he was interrupted by the banging of the saloon door. There stood Ella in her riding clothes, her face flushed from what had obviously been a hard ride.

"Hello, girl," said Boss Quinn quietly. "See ya in a few minutes, Sam."

Sam took the hint. Ella advanced on her father, her eyes flashing.

"Father, what do you mean by all this?"

Boss Quinn looked at her coolly and deliberately refilled his glass.

"Ella," he said at length. "A saloon ain't no place for a daughter of mine."

"I hardly think, Father," said Ella icily, " with men trying to kill each other out there, this is the time to give me lessons on etiquette."

"An' it's hardly the time for you to come questionin' me!"

"I've every right," said Ella. "Lee Royle is in the Good Luck Saloon, surrounded by your hired gunmen. Don't you realise he saved my life, or has it escaped your memory?"

"No," said Boss Quinn. "I'm grateful to him."

"You've a strange way of showing gratitude. Call your men off at once."

"Ella, honey," said Boss Quinn slowly. "I guess it's hard for you to understand, but it's not as easy as that any more. Look at it this way. Lee Royle saved you. But he didn't know who you were. He'd never met you before. He just saved a girl from a fire. And he's a good guy to do that. But he happens to be on the other side.

"Now when that fire was burning he didn't know you were my daughter an' I guess it wouldn't have made no difference to him if he had. But since then he's murdered Pete Montana, he's sided with the men who started the fire, the men who shot my cattle, the men who'd like to overrun the Circle-Star and put wire across the range, the Johnnies-come-lately who think they're entitled to the range as a birthright, after I've tamed it. I'm the one who's been attacked, Ella, not them. If Lee Royle goes on their side, he's the enemy.

"But I'll tell you this, I've tried to do what I could. I tried to have him arrested for the shootin' an' then maybe we could see he had a trial fair an' square, but Silver Bend seems to have lost its marshal, temporarily anyway. An' if I told my men to stop fightin' they'd be shot down themselves."

While he had been talking at length, Ella had been watching the harsh features of her father, her face changing from the flush from hard riding to a pale, suppressed fury.

"These are just words, Father," she snapped. "Making excuses for yourself because, in the bottom of your heart, you know you're wrong. You've been Boss of the Circle-Star so long that you believe you are above the law. You try and run everybody according to your word, including me."

"That's a hard remark, Ella," Boss Quinn replied. "Someday maybe you'll see it my way, mebbe."

"I'll never see it your way, Father," she retorted, "I may be your daughter, but I don't take after you and that hurts you, doesn't it? I know you'd rather have had a son, someone you could have handed the Circle-Star on to, someone who would rule it as ruthlessly as you've done ..."

"Ella," said Boss Quinn. " This isn't the time for us to feud. Go back home an' ... an' I'll be back as soon as I can."

"Wash the blood off your hands before you come back," said Ella. "You frighten me now, Father. At last I begin to see why Mother left you."

From down the street came a fusillade of shots.

"I can't fight a war and you," said Boss Quinn, his face suddenly weary. "Let me deal with these varmints an' then I'll put it right with you."

He strode to the door and vanished into the glare of Main Street.

Royle was back down in the saloon. There had been a lull in the firing but now, as if by a preconceived signal, bullets began slamming into the walls of the saloon. Instinct told him there was new danger to face. Suddenly he felt a sensation of release, as though a heavy weight had been removed from him. Standing in the bar amidst the drifting lace of gun smoke he felt strangely exalted. Events had moved very fast in the last few hours, but now the realisation that he had avenged his brother suddenly caught up with him. But it was not only this. It was that once more he had his gun in his hand, once more he was living with the strange, sick excitement of gunplay and once more, for the first time in years, he felt he held his destiny in his right hand.

There was a twisted half grin on his face as he looked round the saloon at his companions crouched at

96

their posts by the windows, at the barman pouring himself out yet another drink, at the shattered glass on the floor and the mangled piano piled up against the door. He smiled, like a man who has remembered the thrill of his first and greatest love after a long and arid time. Frontier in hand, Royle moved over to one of the windows and crouched down beside Ulysses Shepherd.

"They sure are pumpin' lead into this old place," said Ulysses. "I wonder if they're gonna try and rush us?"

Before Royle could reply there was a drumming of hooves. To their amazement they saw a rider galloping down Main Street. As he swept past the Good Luck Saloon in a cloud of dust he appeared to be paying out a rope which was coiled in large loops round his saddle horn.

Several shots from the besieged men whistled close to him but then within seconds he was out of range, and the only signs of his mad gallop was the floating dust and the rope which now moved snake-like along the dirt of Main Street.

"Now what the hell did Slim Springfield want to do that for?" Ulysses exclaimed.

"Who's Slim Springfield?"

"One of Boss Quinn's hired guns," was the reply. "He's got a pretty bad reputation. He's mighty slick on the draw with his left hand. It fools a lot of people. He's got a funny nickname. They call him The Burner."

"Why is that?" asked Royle.

Ulysses didn't reply. He was watching the rope which was now moving as though it had a life of its own. It rose several inches above the level of the street, then swung closer to the Good Luck Saloon as Circle-Star men, safely out of sight, dragged it into position. The men at the front of the Good Luck Saloon watched it with fascination.

"Now what in tarnation can they be up to?" asked

Jason Shepherd, as the rope jerked taut.

"I dunno," said Royle. "But I sure don't like the looks of it."

Firing had died down again. Suddenly there was a yell from the roof. Royle risked ducking his head round the window frame and realised the function of the rope. Attached to it was a large wagon, piled high with straw which had been set alight. That the rope was being pulled by unseen hands so that the wagon would roll down the street until it collided with the front of the Good Luck Saloon, transforming the drought-dry timbers of the building into an inferno. The besieged men would be forced to leap into the Circle-Star line of fire, or be burnt to death horribly.

Inside the saloon Royle ran over to the barman.

"You gotta knife?" he demanded. The barman looked at him wide-eyed. Now he had escaped into intoxication it seemed that he was unable to comprehend.

"Gimme a knife, damn you, gimme a knife," yelled Royle.

The barman slowly reached under the bar and even more slowly brought out a bowie which had been removed from a patron who had partaken of too much alcoholic refreshment and then waved the weapon about in an unbecoming manner.

Royle seized it and ran over to a window, knocking aside the barricade of furniture and tables. He jumped through the empty frame in a flying leap and landed on all fours beside the rope which was now snaking past him.

Seizing it, he was partially dragged along while he slashed at it with the knife. Looking up, about a hundred or so yards down the street, he saw a group of Circle-Star men pulling vigorously. He kept slashing, but the rope slipped through his fingers. Turning his head he saw the hay cart, its load now roaring with flame, only about twenty feet away. Another few seconds and it would crash into the veranda of the Good Luck.

Now he clung to the rope with desperation. As he was towed through the dust he was no longer hacking at the hemp but sawing at it. This method was more successful. He was hardly aware of the spurts of dirt as bullets struck the road around him. A moment later there was somebody standing above him. Ulysses Shepherd, a rifle at his hip, was firing back at the Circle-Star men. The final strand parted. A cheer went up from the men in the Good Luck Saloon. Royle dropped the knife and scrambled to his feet.

He saw the wagon was still rolling. He raced to it and clamped the brake on. Ulysses followed him, firing down the street at the group of men who had tumbled over like a tug-of-war team.

From round the corner of a harness shop appeared Sam Cash. It was like a moment frozen in time. Ulysses was down on one knee, his rifle spurting flame down the street. Royle, whose Frontier had remained bolstered while he had been wrestling with the brake, could feel the heat of the blazing straw blistering the skin on his face. Before he could draw, he saw Sam point his Navy Colt at him – then deliberately swing it away.

The pistol fired and Sam Cash ducked back behind the wall of the harness shop. Ulysses Shepherd gave a high-pitched scream, dropped his rifle, staggering to his feet in agony. His hands clawing at his stomach. Royle leapt forward and put his arm out to support the reeling youth.

"My belly," he moaned. "It's busted open. Can't somebody do something?" He slumped forward on his knees. Royle put his hands under his armpits and began dragging him. A trail of blood marked their progress towards the Good Luck Saloon.

Down the street Slim Springfield raised his rifle with calm deliberation and took careful aim. He grinned wolfishly, the tip of his tongue licking his sharp and twisted teeth. He knew that within a second he would have the exquisite pleasure of snuffing out a human life.

CHAPTER 10

The muscles of Slim Springfield's forefinger began to contract. His eye saw the tip of the foresight and the distant figure of Lee Royle were in direct line. Before the same eye appeared a hand, a hand that grasped the barrel and pointed it downwards. The finger, however, continued the contraction. In the breech the powder exploded and the bullet dug a furrow in the dust a few yards from his feet.

Slim Springfield snarled like an animal deprived of its prey at the last minute. Eyes blazing, he swung round to see the person who had saved the life of Lee Royle was Ella Quinn. For a moment he gazed at her, white-faced with fury, unable to find words while she regarded him with a look of haughty contempt.

"Goddam it, Miss Quinn," he exclaimed. "Whose side you on?"

"Work it out for yourself, Mister Springfield," she replied. "It ain't right to shoot a man when he's helping a wounded comrade."

Slim Springfield endeavoured to bite back the words of anger which were flooding to his mouth but before anything further could be said, Boss Quinn cut in.

"Ella, this ain't no place for you," he said. "Ride back to the Circle-Star an' wait there till I come. This is men's work and you durned well don't understand it."

For a moment Ella's eyes switched from Springfield to her father.

"I understand it all right," she said quietly, and turning, walked away to where her horse was tethered.

"Sometimes I think I reared a wildcat," Boss Quinn growled, not without a touch of pride. He turned to the men who had been watching the scene with aloof expressions.

"Okay, boys," he said. "It'll be nightfall soon an' I want that nest of settlers cleared out by then. Remember, I'm buyin' the ammunition."

At the other end of Main Street, unaware of the drama that had just occurred, Lee Royle dragged Ulysses Shepherd up the steps of the saloon. Willing hands carried him inside and he was laid down on the floor. A rolled-up coat was placed under his head for a pillow.

"Thanks, fellas," said Jason Shepherd. "We'll look after him. Get back to your posts. They may try an' rush us." He and Royle bent over the moaning boy. He was pressing his hands to his stomach with blood oozing between his fingers so it appeared as though he was wearing red gloves.

"I feel damn bad, Jason," he managed to mutter. "I didn't ever know it could feel as bad as this."

"Just you hang on, kid," said Jason in a choking voice. "We'll get the doc to you in a couple of shakes an' he'll make everything right again."

Ulysses looked round wildly for a moment and then his eyes focused once more on his brother's face.

"I guess there won't be time for that, Jason," he said. "I feel as though I'm drainin' away somehow. But I know you'll even it up for me – won't you?"

"I swear to God I'll do that, Ulysses," said Jason, the tears trickling down his cheeks. "They'll pay ten times over for what they done to you this afternoon."

The boy tried to smile his thanks to his brother but the smile suddenly contracted into a fearful grimace. Within seconds, the eyes began to glaze.

"He's gone, Jason," said Royle softly. "Fact is, even if we had been able to get a doc he wouldn't have had a chance."

"He was only sixteen," muttered Jason. "Oh my God, he was only sixteen."

102

They moved the dead boy into a corner of the saloon, laying a blanket over him. Without a word Jason picked up his gun and took up his position at the window again. There was an anguished expression on his face and no one dared to speak to him. Royle went up the stairs again to the roof, the smoke of the burning hay wagon making his eyes smart. It seemed the siege had returned to sniping. Bullets whistled overhead or plunked into the woodwork of the building, while the men of the Silver Bend Cattlemen's Protection Association contented themselves with firing only when they saw a movement or a puff of smoke.

It was now late afternoon and each defender began to wonder what would happen when night fell.

"Tell me," said Royle to the man who was stretched out beside him. "Why is Slim Springfield known as The Burner?"

"Before he joined up with Boss Quinn he used to carry a gun for the Santa Fe Ring," explained the man, who was known simply as Otis. "Whenever there was trouble Slim Springfield was there. Waal, as you know, the Santa Fe Ring is a syndicate of some of the biggest cattle barons, and when the homesteaders tried to come in they saw to it they were warned off the range. Warnin' 'em off was Slim Springfield's speciality. He an' his gang would ride up at night and surround a settler's shack. Some of 'em would creep up with oil or blastin' powder and set it alight. The rest just sat round in a circle, pumping a few shots into the homestead to add to the fun. Sometimes they'd let the nesters come out, sometimes they'd keep them inside with their gunfire. That's how Slim Springfield got the name."

Before Royle could reply there came the ringing tone of a bugle followed by the drumming of hooves. Down Main Street, past the smoking wreck of the hay wagon, galloped a troop of cavalry behind a fluttering pennant. At the rear of the column was a light covered cart bouncing along the dusty street at top speed. Ignoring spasmodic shots exchanged between the Protection Association men and the Circle-Star followers, the cavalry halted in a cloud of dust halfway between the Good Luck Saloon and the Silver Lode. Their appearance had been so quick and dramatic the firing died and both sides gazed at them in astonishment. Looking down at the blue-uniformed troopers, the man who'd been telling Royle about Slim Springfield muttered: "Goddam Yankees."

At the back of the column several troopers had hastily unloaded a Gatling gun from the cart and assembled it on a stand. The rest of the men sat on their lathered horses, their carbines ready. The leader of the troop wheeled his horse so he could address the men in the besieged Good Luck Saloon.

"I'm Captain Powers," he shouted, his hand momentarily straying up to the black patch over his eye, "and I have brought my men to stop you goddam loco coyotes from murderin' each other. I was ordered over here by telegraph from the War Department. It seems they don't want Silver Bend to turn into another Lincoln. And I'm gonna see that that doesn't happen. Now I don't give a damn who's right or who's wrong. All I care about is that you stop throwin' lead at each other. If you want to carry on shootin' let me tell you this. My men have had a long, hard ride because of you and they're bad-tempered and they've got itchy fingers. And the other thing is, we've got a Gatling gun here. It spits bullets at the rate of a thousand rounds a minute and I happen to know that Trooper Wilson there would love to use it."

"I sure would, Captain," responded the Gatling gun-ner, drawing back his trail-cracked lips. "This gun could chop Silver Bend apart."

Captain Powers steadied his horse, which was inclined to skitter, and resumed. "I want all of you to come out into the street," he yelled. "This town is now under military law and you'll do as I tell you." There was no movement. Each side was waiting to see what the other would do.

"All right, then," shouted the Captain. "I want your leaders to come out here and make it fast, otherwise you'll learn what real trouble is."

Jason Shepherd walked down the steps of the Good Luck Saloon, past the curious stares of the troopers and up to Captain Powers. "I'm Jason Shepherd," he said, "and I'm president of the Silver Bend Cattlemen's Protection Association."

The trim military officer looked at him with a slight sneer of contempt. "From now on, Shepherd, I'm all the protection that's needed in these parts."

From the other end of the street stumped Boss Quinn.

"I'm glad to see law and order has arrived, Captain," he said. "The reason for this trouble today is the murder of my foreman."

"Who did it?"

"Man by the name of Lee Royle. He's in the saloon there."

"It was a fair fight," protested Jason Shepherd. "You can't arrest him when Montana had his gun out."

"Any witnesses?"

Hyatt, the man Royle had wounded on his first visit to Silver Bend, stepped forward. "I don't care a cuss for the Circle-Star," he said, "but I'll testify Royle shot Pete Montana down in cold blood."

"All right," snapped Captain Powers. "Where's the town marshal?"

With a sheepish look on his face Marshal Dolan sidled from his office.

"Marshal," said Captain Powers, "I'm gonna hand Lee Royle over to you in a minute and I want you to lock him up for safe keepin' until we get this mess sorted out."

"There's just one thing, Captain," Jason Shepherd gritted. "My kid brother is lying dead in the Good Luck Saloon. He was shot down by one of this bunch."

"Well, we'd better get him too," said Powers. "We'll hold them both as hostages. Come on out, you men."

Royle walked into the street and stood in front of the Captain. From the opposite end came Sam Cash.

"Is this what you want me to do?" he asked Boss Quinn.

"That's right, Sam," said Boss Quinn. "We'll get you outa here plenty fast, don't fret. You were shootin' in self-defence."

Sam Cash grinned at Royle. "Looks like we're gonna share a cell, fella."

"Marshal," said Captain Powers, "take these two men and put 'em in your cell."

"Yeah, anythin' you say, Cap'n," mumbled the marshal. "Come on, boys. Don't give me no trouble and I'll treat you right."

He led the way to his office. Sam Cash and Royle followed behind, both watched by the men who a few minutes before had been engaged in annihilating each other. Inside the marshal's office the men unstrapped their gunbelts and handed their weapons to the marshal who put them in a cupboard.

"I ain't gonna share no cell with that drunken bum there," exploded Sam Cash and he pointed to the old prospector behind the bars.

"Who're you callin' a drunken bum, you gun-happy varmint," exploded Ted Hawkins. "I may be a bum but I ain't drunk – wish to Gawd I was. It's awful dry in here."

"Well, I ain't goin' in that cell while he's there Royle. You'd better give him a free pardon, Marshal. In fact, I'll go so far as to pay his fine."

Ignoring them all, the marshal unhappily unlocked the door of the cell. "Go on," he said to the old gold hunter. "*Vamos!*"

"How about a shot for the road?" suggested Hawkins, with the endless optimism of the drunk. "I know you got plenty of firewater stashed away." The marshal ignored him.

"In you go, boys," he said. Resignedly Royle walked inside. Sam followed him, pausing at the door to say mock-heroically: "Farewell, Freedom." The door slammed shut with a metallic clang, a clang that echoed dismally through the corridors of Royle's memory, reviving his hatred for locks and bars.

"Now don't give me no trouble, boys," pleaded the marshal. "You stay nice and peaceful an' I'll see you get good grub."

"It's a deal, Marshal," said Sam Cash. "The boss'll spring me pretty soon, but while I'm here I'll deal you a free hand if the chuck is fit for a man with my kinda appetite."

Outside in the dying afternoon the Circle-Star men rode back towards their ranch in a body, while the members of the Silver Bend Cattlemen's Protection Association dispersed to their homes. Captain Powers had ordered a curfew, threatening to shoot on sight anyone who was found on the street after sunset. The cavalry men took up their positions, half of them leading their horses to the corral behind the livery stables while the rest guarded Main Street with their carbines. Soon the town was deserted and as the darkness began to fall Captain Powers gave the order to his men to bivouac, and marched into the marshal's office. To his surprise the prisoners were sitting on their low bunks, facing each other. A box between them, on which lay an old blanket, acted as a card table.

"You seem friendly enough, seein' as you was out

to kill each other this afternoon," Captain Powers commented sourly.

Sam Cash looked up with a grin. "Ah, we're really best of pals, General," he drawled. "'Specially since I've just won my fancy spurs back offa him."

CHAPTER 11

The buzzard hung in the sky as though suspended by a fine wire. The only hint of life was an occasional flexing of its heavy wings to catch the upward flowing currents of hot air which rose endlessly from the drought-dammed earth, or the swivelling of its obscenely bald head as its telescopic eyes probed the barren land for a sign of death. A couple of miles to the south there was another black dot in the sky, and the buzzard kept a watchful eye on this too. It was its mate, and if it began to plummet earthwards the buzzard would follow to get its share of carrion.

To the north the bird could see the distant huddle of square buildings representing Silver Bend, and further still, almost on the edge of the horizon, was the great bulk of The Plateau. These days the buzzard had learned to avoid The Plateau. There were cattle there in plenty, but they were healthy cattle thanks to the strip of glittering water that winked at the sun from the main valley. The buzzard knew his food was to be found on the open rangeland, along the black tracks of dried mud that had once been the veins carrying life-giving water to the small ranches whose insignificant houses could be seen here and there on the vast plain.

For some time the eye scavenger's eye had been focused on a cow directly below. It had been wandering aimlessly in circles ever since the sun had risen, and now an instinct told the bird that death was close. Its wings folded back and it began the long fast descent.

Far below the buzzard Jed Morrow watched the cow as it struggled round and round in smaller and smaller circles, its eyes glazed and its swollen tongue hanging from its dry mouth. Sometimes it would raise its head to the pitiless sky and attempt to voice its protest against nature for condemning it to its wretched plight.

Jed sat on hot rock and lit a smoke, all the time studying the movements of the dying animal. To his eyes it was not the death throes of a cow he was watching, but the end of his own particular dream. The cow symbolised the defeat of a smallholder who had staked everything on coming West, who had invested all his money, labour and the future of his family in trying to wrest a living from the new land. After several tough seasons while he was getting established, it seemed he was going to win through, but when the drought had come it had gradually but remorselessly undone all his work and whittled down the herd he had striven so hard to build up.

Mary had been at him to quit for weeks now. She wanted to load up the wagon with their sticks of furniture and hit the trail back East, especially since the kids were getting sick because they weren't getting the right food any more. But, Jed had argued, what could they go back to? He felt he would rather try and hang on than have to face the ordeal of starting all over again ... he knew that he could not start again. Something had busted inside him, the spirit that had brought him here was gone, dried up like his creek. He was a shell of a man, and he knew it.

He tried to pacify Mary by saying that the drought could not last, that it was a matter of seeing it through, that next year the price of beef would soar and they would be all right again, but it was hard to convince her against the background sound of crying children and the lowing of thirst-crazed stock.

Now, as he watched the cow with strange detachment and drew on his smoke, he said to himself, "If Mary's right – I can't go on another day. I don't know what will happen to us if we leave, but I don't care. All I know is that I'm beat." He rose to his feet, picking up the old rifle that had lain beside him. The metal was so hot that he shifted his grip to the wooden stock.

He began to trudge over the powdery earth in the direction of the shack he had built with his own hands just a few years ago when his hopes were so fresh. The cow, now on its knees, gave a pitiful moan. Something akin to pity stopped Jed in his tracks. He felt a fellow feeling for the beast. Like himself, it was the victim of something outside its understanding. Jed walked over to it, placed the muzzle of his rifle against its forehead and jerked the trigger.

As the sound of the shot died away an ugly black shape swept down and stood close to the dead animal, surveying the scene with its greedy eyes. To Jed it seemed the personification of disaster.

"I don't care if I am low on cartridges," he muttered. He swung up the barrel and fired again. The black-feathered omen of death exploded into a heap of feathers. In sudden fury Jed strode over to the bird, kicking it and then grinding it into the soil with his large work boot.

When he reached the shack he called out: "Mary, get packin' – we're pullin' out."

"It's taken you long enough to see sense," his wife grumbled, as she tried to pacify a squawling baby. She saw there was blood on her husband's boot, but she did not have enough interest to ask him about it. Out on the plain the dead buzzard's mate had begun to peck at the eyes of the cow.

Slim Springfield felt good. It was the day after the battle of Main Street, and now the burning anger that had filled him when Ella Quinn had spoiled his chance to kill Lee Royle had abated. The reason was that he was engaged on a special job for Boss Quinn, and it was a job very much to his taste, taking him back to the happy days when he had carried a gun as an agent for the Santa Fe

Ring.

The morning sun was already scorching and a runnel of sweat ran down his forehead from under his city-style derby. His two companions, following him along the narrow, dusty trail that twisted through patches of mesquite, were dressed for the range and therefore more comfortable. But it was a point of honour with Slim Springfield that he always dressed in a way that would not look out of place on the more fashionable sidewalks of New York. It was a shame his heavy revolver and its broad cartridge-filled belt spoilt the sartorial effect, but then a guy could not have everything. One had to compromise for the sake of one's art.

At length the three Circle-Star riders reached a mean-looking shack, the home of a small settler. In front of it was an old wagon and Jed Morrow was in the process of hitching up his mules. The animals stood with their heads hanging down, their ribs almost coming through their scarred hides. At the jingle of the riders Jed paused, and his wife appeared at the door.

"You Jed Morrow?" asked Slim Springfield as he drew up and lounged forward on the horn of his saddle. His lips curved back in a look of contempt as he let his gaze travel slowly over the ragged figure of the settler.

"That's what I was named," said Jed in a surly tone. "What's it to you?"

"We've come over from the Circle-Star," said Slim. "I got a message for you from the Boss."

"Can't say I'm interested in what he's got to say, but spill it anyways."

"Waal, the Boss is worried about you little guys. He knows you been hard hit by the drought, so he's willing to make you an offer. He'll buy up your land if you sign it over to him and quit."

"How much is he payin'?" demanded Mary Morrow.

"It's a durned generous offer," Slim replied with a humourless grin. "Twenty-five cents an acre."

Jed Morrow turned and looked at his wife uncertainly, but she gazed directly up at Slim Springfield.

"That's a loco offer," she said. "Now, git off our property."

"It's you that's loco, ma'am," said Slim. "I can see you already decided to quit..."

"We ain't quittin', mister," said Jed, turning back to face the Circle-Star men with a new, determined look on his face. "Sure, Boss Quinn would like to buy up the whole range at twenty-five cents an acre – that's why he's cut the water, but we ain't quittin'. Like my wife said, I'd be obliged if you'd get off our land."

"What you tryin' to do, Morrow? Force the price up? Why, I can see by that wagon that you were gettin' ready to quit."

"We weren't quittin', mister," said Mary Morrow. "Jed was takin' the wagon into Silver Bend to sell it –"

The three horsemen roared with laughter.

"You sure believe in miracles if you think you could sell that there wagon," said Slim. "Now, look, fella, we're offerin' a good price. I got it here in cash –" he touched his saddle pack, "... all you got to do is sign this here paper." He brought it from an inside pocket of his elegant coat.

"Lemme see that paper," demanded Jed. Slim passed it down to him. Jed scanned it briefly. It meant nothing to him as he was illiterate, but he made a show of reading and then tore it into fragments.

"That's what I think of Boss Quinn's offer," he said.

"An' that goes for me, too, mister," said Mary.

Slim sat silent a long minute. Things were working out exactly as he had hoped.

At last he said slowly: "You gonna be very sorry

113

you ripped up that paper."

"You can't scare me," retorted Jed. "You Circle-Star *hombres* don't own this land. Pete Montana tried to push the preacher an' look what happened to him. An' now I hear tell the cavalry is in Silver Bend, so the days when you bossed the range are over."

"You're treadin' on your luck, Morrow," said Slim in a silky voice. "Boys, set the shack alight – "

The two riders began to dismount. With a curse Jed Morrow turned to his wagon and snatched up his rifle from beside the driver's seat.

"First one to take a step forward is a dead man," he snapped. His voice was firm, but the gun trembled in his hand. He had never pointed a gun at a fellow human being before.

"Go on, boys," Slim ordered. "He's too yeller to use that squirrel-shooter."

The two men advanced towards the settler. Seeing that his gun was having no effect on them, he fired, the shot whining over their heads as he had intended. Next second the gun, that had magically appeared in Slim's left hand, crashed. Jed pitched forward with a scream. The bullet had smashed his kneecap.

"Okay, boys, let's leave him to it," said Slim. "The cavalry will be out later on, ma'am," he said to the white-faced Mary who was clutching the door post. "The charge will be attempted murder. The State Governor ain't gonna have much sympathy with you goddamned settlers when he hears that you shoot at us when we try to help you in your hour of need."

Slim's henchmen swung back into their saddles and began to canter down the trail.

* * *

Sam Cash looked up from the fan of cards he held in his hand. "What's new, Marshal?" he asked, as Dolan

114

walked into his office, holding a new bottle of Old Vermont by the neck.

"I hope you aim to share that there rotgut with me. I sure could use a shot – this fella Royle has just won them silver spurs back."

"Silver Bend's quiet," replied the marshal, ignoring Cash's latter remark. "That Captain Powers' got his men patrollin' all over, and he's given an order that's agin the law to wear shootin' irons in town. Soon as anyone rides in they have to hand over their hardware to the soldiers, and they don't get it back till they leave town."

"It must be mighty peaceful, then," sighed Sam Cash.

"Sure is," agreed the marshal. "An' it's likely to keep that way until the judge has come over an' fixed you two guys."

"They can stop trouble in Silver Bend," said Royle thoughtfully. "But there ain't enough men to patrol the whole range. I'm bettin' there'll be a lot more trouble before that judge turns up."

"Well, you won't be mixed up in it," said Marshal Dolan. "An' I reckon you ought to be thankful you're both locked up good an' safe. I guess some of the Circle-Star boys would like to have a few words with you Royle. An' as for you, Cash, if it weren't for the soldiers there'd be a lynchin' mob outside right now. Ulysses Shepherd was a popular guy an' you done a bad thing when you plugged him."

"Now listen to that," complained Sam Cash in offended tones. "It was a gun battle – am I supposed not to fire at popular guys when the lead is flyin'? It was a fair 'nough killin'."

"Who cares about fairness, Sam," said Royle. "The fact is you belong to the Circle-Star, an' that's a good enough reason for the settlers wantin' to invite you to a neck-tie party."

Sam Cash drew his hand down his bearded cheek thoughtfully. "My old Pappy usta say I'd end up on the end of a rope," he said. "Maybe he'll be proved right."

"Not with them soldiers about," said Marshal Dolan, helping himself to a tot. "They've got that there Gatlin' gun fixed up outside in the street. They reckon that could hold back an army."

"I guess it could," said Royle. "They say that if General Custer had taken his Gatlins along he'd been alive today. Custer never liked 'em, reckoned they were a hindrance so he left 'em behind."

"Pick up them cards," said Sam Cash. "I wanna get them spurs back."

Out in Main Street a tumbleweed rolled erratically past the Good Luck Saloon and the small knot of men who were gathering there. Inside the bullet scarred walls more men were taking quick drinks without conversation. Jason Shepherd appeared at the door, his face looking grey and harsh.

"All right, boys," he said, "let's get going."

From the back of the saloon a black coffin was carried and laid on a cart, then the cortege of Ulysses Shepherd moved off slowly down the street. Some of the men following walked awkwardly because there was no longer a familiar weight on their thighs. Troopers, with their carbines in their hands, watched the procession in silence. Captain Powers stepped out of the Silver Lode, where he had made his headquarters, and looked on coldly as the squeaking vehicle and its straggling followers went by.

The procession headed along the trail leading out of Silver Bend for about a quarter of a mile before it reached the small cemetery. Surrounded by a rough picket fence, it contained about two score of rough headboards. Some just proclaimed the name of the deceased and the date of his death, others had a few brief but graphic

116

details, such as "Killed by Indians" or "Shot down in a fair fight".

The coffin was carried through the gateway to a spot where a couple of friends of the Shepherds' were digging a grave. Most of the mourners sat in the shade of some stunted trees while the work continued, but Jason Shepherd stood alone, gazing sombrely at the distant silhouette of The Plateau.

The onlookers drew on their cigarettes, but said very little. The one event, apart from yesterday's battle, which would have provided conversation was the flight of Jonathan Q. Nimrod, yet his name was not mentioned. Perhaps it was because each one had secretly known that his columns of chemical smoke would fail, that each had handed over his few dollars for an illusion, and now the illusion was shattered there was resignation rather than anger. They knew the rainmaker had not tricked them, they had tricked themselves, and yet in doing so they had not lost completely. For a few days there had been hope in Silver Bend.

"I reckon it's about deep enough now, Jason," called one of the diggers.

The coffin was carried over to the grave and Jason stood up tall in front of it.

"I reckon there's gotta be a few words said over my brother," he said. "I wish the preacher was here to say 'em, but he's ill with a gunshot wound, so I'm gonna say them myself."

The men gathered round now, and out of respect for the dead youth they had ground their cigarettes into the dust with their heels.

Jason looked up into the cloudless sky as though searching for the right words. Then he looked down at the coffin.

"Ulysses, you was only a kid when you was shot down yesterday," he said. "If that bullet hadn't found you,

117

you might have growed to be an old man with kids of your own, an' grandchildren – Waal, it wasn't to be. I don't know why, an' you don't know why, but you are dead an' though I feel I oughta say something good an' hopeful, I can't. Maybe the sky pilot could've said things that wouldn't make it so bad, but I can't. You're dead, Ulysses, an' it's a goddamned shame. Amen."

The rest muttered an amen and looked down at their boots.

The silence was followed by the creak of the gate. Slowly the men turned. Another party was entering the cemetery, carrying two coffins. The Circle-Star had come to bury Ford Vance and Pete Montana.

CHAPTER 12

"Gawd, it's hotter'n the inside of a stove," complained Sam Cash. "Ain't you hot, *compadre*?"

"Yeah, but it don't cool me down none talkin' about it," replied Royle. "An' I'll give you some advice for free – pacin' up an' down won't help you none. Just lie on your bed an' think about nothin'."

"Aw, you're just bein' ornery 'cause I got them spurs back – an' a couple of dollars besides."

"Ain't so, Sam. It's just that I'm an old hand at this. I seen guys go crazy pacin' up an' down, complainin' about the grub, lookin' through the bars an' fussin' theirselves up. Only thing is to get right inside yourself an' just be a big nothin' until one day the warder comes with his big key an' lets you out into the world again ..."

Sam Cash sat down on his bed, listlessly picked up the grimy pack of cards and started a half-hearted game of patience. What Royle had said had interested him, he wanted to question him about his experiences, but a certain inbuilt courtesy prevented him. Royle would talk when he felt like it, or perhaps he would never talk about it. Either way, his past was his own private possession and not something acquaintances could probe to pass away the time.

Sam Cash threw down the pasteboards. "Where's that goddam marshal?" he demanded. "I asked for water half an hour ago an' he ain't come back. Mebbe the town's right out of water now. Mebbe whisky is the only liquid left. Think on that, old Dolan will have to keep pumpin' Red Eye into us or we'll cash our chips ... an' if we did that think how mad the judge'd be after comin' so far to see us."

"More like old Dolan's pumpin' Red Eye into himself," Royle said.

The two men sat in silence for a while, watching with unnatural concentration the journey of a large bluebottle up the cell wall. Suddenly the insect, perhaps uncomfortably aware of the four eyes following its progress, vibrated its wings and buzzed through the barred window into the glare of the sun-blasted day.

"Wish I was a durned fly," murmured Sam Cash. "Say, Lee, what say we escape?"

"Not a hope," Royle replied. "They got the militia all round. I bet that fella with the Gatlin' gun would like nothin' better than to use us for targets."

"I sure hate that gun," Sam Cash declared. "It don't give nobody a chance. With a Colt it is a question of speed an' skill, it's man to man like fightin' should always be. But that durned contraption spews out bullets like hailstones comin' down from the sky. It don't need aim or anythin'. Any blamed coyote could mow down a regiment with it. It should never have been made, but I reckon some day all wars will be fought with them things, an' the winnin' side will be the one that can afford the most ammunition."

"You could be right, Sam. But maybe someone said the same thing about the first sixgun."

"Aw, that's different."

The door of the marshal's office opened and Captain Powers marched in, followed by the shambling figure of Dolan.

Royle and Sam Cash continued lounging on their beds.

"On your feet, didn't you hear me the first time?" the captain shouted.

"Seems to me the military has arrived," remarked Sam Cash.

"Sure does sound that way," agreed Royle. "It's a

nice uniform, and I reckon that sword is plumb elegant."

"Makes me feel kinda safe to know the army's with us," went on Sam. "They're a brave lot of fellas, Lee, an' they got Gatlin' guns an' all."

"Cut that out," Powers snarled in a voice that could make veterans of the Indian wars tremble. "Any sass from you bums an' I'll haul you out of here an' give you a taste of field punishment."

At these words Sam Cash appeared to be very frightened. He leapt to his feet and did a parody of a military salute, pretending to knock himself in the eye.

"This salutin's goddam hard," he confided to Royle who remained sprawled on his bed, watching the antics of his cell mate with a hint of amusement in his faded blue eyes.

"Trouble with salutin' is you are inclined to do yourself harm," Sam Cash continued. "Ever noticed how many one-eyed soldiers there are, Lee? It all comes with this here salutin'."

Powers' hand began to travel towards his eye patch before he gained control of himself and gripped the hilt of his sword.

"You son of a bitch," he gritted, walking close to the bars. "You may think you're mighty smart, but by God I'll do all I can to wipe that smile off your ugly faces. I'll look forward to the jokes you crack when the judge says you gotta swing – I'll enjoy hearin' your remarks about one-eyed soldiers when the hemp collar is fittin' snug round your lousy necks. That's if the lynch mob don't get you first. After what happened today they're ripe for a lynchin', and I won't try too hard to stop 'em. Marshal, keep these men on bread an' water."

"Yippee," cried Sam Cash. "We're gonna get some water. Now ain't that kind of the nice captain – I've been on an' on to this blamed old cuss of a marshal for water for hours and it takes a hoss soldier to come an' save me

121

from thirst."

Without a word the captain turned on his heel and stalked out.

"I guess we've lost a friend," murmured Sam Cash, flopping back on to his bed. "You heard the man, Marshal.. . he ordered us to have some water. Get it pronto."

"Okay, boys," muttered Marshal Dolan. "I was gettin' you some when that fella came along. I'll get some now, but it'll cost you. I reckon the price is a quarter a bottle."

With a gesture of contempt Royle flung a coin through the bars on to the office floor.

"I sometimes find it hard to figure why the Lord created buzzards and marshals," said Sam Cash.

Lying back with his hat down over his eyes, he began to sing a prison song in a surprisingly pleasant voice:

> *There are bars cross my window,*
> *An' bars cross my door,*
> *An' bars cross my heart*
> *'Cause I see you no more.*
>
> *For what is the sunshine, an' what are the stars*
> *If you only see 'em through steel prison bars –*
>
> *You swore when I left you*
> *You would always wait,*
> *That your love would be with me*
> *Inside this grim gate.*
>
> *But the months have gone by*
> *With never a sign*
> *Of a letter, or token*
> *That once you were mine.*

I know I was guilty –
I'm bowed down with shame,
An' I'm servin' my time
For savin' your name.

For you needed the money
I took with my gun,
An' now I am payin'
For the wrong I have done.

I remember you weepin'
When they took me away,
But another was with you
The very next day.

An' maybe I'll meet him
One day in the yard,
If he goes like me
An' loves you too hard.

For you are a woman
With a heart icy cold,
An' all that you love
Is the glitter of gold.

Lee Royle joined in softly in the final chorus:

For what is the sunshine an' what are the stars
If only you see 'em through steel prison bars.

"Danged if I can understand you varmints," grumbled Marshal Dolan coming through the door with the full water bottles. "Yesterday you was tryin' to murder each other, today you're singin' like you was the best pals in the world."

"'Course we're pals," Sam Cash laughed. "Don't

123

you think, Marshal, that 'cause we throw a bit of lead in each other's direction, we don't like each other. Why, we been trail mates. Only we're on opposite sides. This silly cuss here has teamed up with them smallholders an' I get my pay from Boss King. Now, a little thing like that ain't enough to start us scrappin' when we're in the caboose. Mebbe if we was to get outa here, we'd be throwin' lead again. Ain't that so?" he said, turning to Royle.

Royle nodded: "That's the way it is." Dolan shook his head in bewilderment. He had expected the two men to have had a stand-up fight by now, and, while he could not appreciate the situation, he was very relieved that he would not be called upon to separate them.

When the two prisoners had slaked their thirst, Sam Cash turned to Dolan who was sitting gloomily at his desk, no doubt mourning the absence of the rainmaker with whom he had secretly hoped to go into partnership. There had been something about the way piles of dollars had appeared to swell the rain fund that had captured his imagination.

"What was the hoss soldier sayin' about somethin' happenin' today that riled folk up? Has there been another shootin'?"

"It was when they was out buryin' Ulysses Shepherd," said Dolan. "Seems like they had just got him planted when up comes the Circle-Star outfit to bury a couple of their boys. Well, nobody on either side was carryin' a gun in his holster. The soldiers had taken 'em all when they rode in, see. An' anyway, I guess both sides figured that a buryin' weren't no place to start the war off again.

"So Boss King just leads his men past Jason Shepherd an' they go over to the other side of the graveyard.

"When it was over an' the Circle-Star was walking back, Boss King suddenly goes up to Jason an' says a few words. Some folk reckon he said somethin' about stopping the war right there an' then, seein' as how three good men had been planted because of it.

"Maybe he said somethin' else – he spoke kinda low. Old Abe Jackson reckoned he told Jason that, if they would forget what'd happened the smallholders could water their cattle on the Circle-Star range – but whatever it was, it didn't make no durned difference, 'cause Jason said that no matter what Boss King said, it wouldn't bring Ulysses back an' to hell with him an' the Circle-Star, an' if it weren't for the military, the Circle-Star would have been wiped out by now. Anyways, their tempers got pretty hot, and Jason takes a swing at Boss King.

"Boss King's an old man, but he's sure a tough old man. He sorta ducked and threw a punch back at Jason that upset his balance. He stumbled back and fell right over his brother's grave. Waal, he jumped up with a curse and was about to rip into Boss King when Slim Springfield pulls out a Derringer he'd had hidden up his sleeve.

"You can join your brother in hell,' he says, but before he can fire Frankie jumps on him from the back an' the little gun goes off pop. Then someone pulls a knife an' a right good fight starts with the Circle-Star boys. It's hardly got goin' when some shots whistle overhead an' there's the hoss soldiers with their carbines. Captain Powers tells 'em to stop, or the next volley'll be for them. So they stop beatin' hell outa each other an' mooch off, sayin' pretty ornery things. The Circle-Star bunch get their ponies an' are just ridin' off when Jed Morrow's eldest kid comes down the trail on one of his old man's mules, sayin' as how his pa's been wounded by Slim Springfield.

"At that it looked like the Silver Bend boys would have gone after the Circle-Star bunch again, but the cavalry gets round them an' Captain Powers says he knows all about it, an' it was self-defence accordin' to witnesses. Right now Jason Shepherd an' his boys are in the Good Luck, an' they're feelin' pretty mean."

"Looks like we missed some fun then," said Sam Cash casually.

"There may be some fun yet," muttered the Marshal. "Give the citizens half a chance an' they'll have you outa jail, Sam, an' at the end of a rope quicker'n you can blink."

"That's the trouble with my business." said Sam Cash. "It gets you unpopular."

* * *

It was an hour before moonrise. Jason Shepherd and four of his men paused on the edge of the great darkness which was the Circle-Star valley, not far from the spot where Luke Muldoon had met his end. Their horses had been tethered further back and now the men were grateful to rest and draw deep breaths after struggling with the heavy loads strapped to their shoulders.

They strained their ears for any sound of danger, but the sickly warm breeze only brought the distant cry of a hoot-owl and the faint wail of a coyote.

"I guess it's all right, fellas," whispered Jason. "They won't expect a night attack from this quarter. If they have any guards, I figure they'll be down the valley some."

The men muttered agreement and began to descend the steep valley wall in the darkness. Often they bit back curses as thorn bushes lacerated them, or sometimes slid down steep slopes in showers of earth and pebbles. After each such falls they would all wait, their ears almost aching with the effort to detect if their enemies had been alerted, but the pounding of their own blood was all they heard.

When they reached the long grass at the bottom, Jason led them unerringly forward. For days he had been coming to The Plateau secretly to spy out the land and plot out the course. Away to the south-west could be seen a faint light marking the position of the Circle-Star ranch building. The small party now headed towards this until they heard the pleasant murmur of water and they found themselves beside the Snowy River.

"Okay, boys, this is where Frankie and I get wet," murmured Jason Shepherd. "Get the charge ready, then you three wait here an' give us cover with your rifles if anythin' goes wrong."

Silently the men unloaded their burdens. Three had been carrying long narrow casks. These were hastily lashed together to make a small raft which was carefully lowered into the water. The other loads consisted of gun cotton charges, wrapped in waterproof material, which were now tied on to the floats. When all was ready, the two men who were going to convey the deadly cargo downstream to the dam placed their six-shooters on top of the explosive and entered the water. They moved slowly to prevent any telltale splashing until the water was up to their necks, then half walking and half swimming they propelled the raft parallel with the bank. The night about them was black, the surface of the water was equally dark. There was nothing except the gentle tug of the current to give them any sense of direction.

"The moon should be comin' up any time now," whispered Jason to Frankie. "We better wait until it gets light enough to see the dam."

"Okay," replied Frankie through chattering teeth. "Funny thing, for weeks I've been dreamin' about water. I guess there was nothing I wanted better'n to jump right into it an' feel it washin' all round me, but now I'd give a month's pay to be back on dry land."

Jason did not reply. He was busy scanning the

darkness for the glow that would herald the moonrise.

"Here it comes," he whispered at last as the darkness over the valley wall seemed to fade and then with surprising speed became a silvery glow. Soon the edge of the moon's disc would appear and then the valley would be flooded with the lunar radiance.

The two men saw they were about twenty feet from the bank on their left. To the right the oily surface of the water stretched away into the velvet shadow which was gradually receding as the moon rose higher.

About five hundred yards ahead of them there was a low dark line which Jason recognised as the top of the dam. "Come on, Frankie," he encouraged, "a few more minutes an' it'll be matchwood."

Once more the raft moved forward. Now they could hear the low splashing of the water jets that sprang from the cracks in the wooden wall. Of the sluices there was no sound, confirming the rumour that Boss King had closed them as a reprisal after the cemetery incident.

As Jason Shepherd manoeuvred the raft further to the right, the feet of the men rarely touched the bottom. They floated with the casks, kicking their legs to keep it moving in the right direction. Soon they found they were nearing the wall of wood that rose a yard above the surface. Then there was a slight bump as the raft touched the heavy beams.

Without a word Frankie took a hook with a light cord and moored the raft securely. Meanwhile Jason reached into an oiled silk bag that had been tied to the charges. From it he took matches. By the bag was the end of a carefully coiled fuse.

He was just about to strike the match when he looked up and saw the figure of a man silhouetted against the moonlight. It moved with agonising slowness along the plank walk that ran along the top of the dam. Frankie saw it too, and wordlessly both men ducked their heads under the water so their faces would not gleam white.

Seconds passed. Lights began to dance before Jason's closed eyes as he fought to hold his breath. When he could stand it no longer he raised his head just long enough to gulp in air and then duck again.

The next-time he raised his head he saw that the guard had passed them and was cautiously treading his way towards the left bank.

"Wait," he hissed to Frankie. They must give the man time to go away, otherwise he might be warned by the spluttering of the fuse.

Five minutes crawled by, then another five. The chill of the water was making both men shudder and Jason's hand was shaking so much it took him several attempts before he got a match alight. This was the most dangerous part in case the flare of the match was seen by some sharp-eyed sentry on the bank. The burning head touched the end of the fuse which began to sizzle.

"Okay, it's away," hissed Jason. The two grasped their pistols and held them above the surface, clumsily paddling with their free hands. As they moved away from the dam Jason panted: "Make for the bank. We don't wanna be sucked through the gap when she blows."

"Sure thing," grunted Frankie. "I can touch the bottom now."

A moment later the saboteurs were wading north, mentally counting off the seconds before the spark which was dancing along the fuse reached the cotton and Boss King's dam would be blasted into splintered wreckage.

* * *

Joe Curtis felt uneasy as he looked at the bulk of the Circle-Star dam in the moonlight. He had just crossed over it from the west bank to the east, a journey he hated. He had one fear in his life, and that was a fear of water. Always at the back of his memory was that terrible day

129

when he was little more than a baby and he had nearly drowned in the local swimming hole. He had fallen in and made a trail of bubbles to the bottom.

Now, when he had nightmares, they were always about long waterweeds twining about his legs and a dim, bubble-spangled world of green where he struggled to no avail, and the black oozy mud sucked his feet, then his legs, and then...

He could not remember the rescue. Probably one of the older kids had dived in and pulled him out. That part was forgotten, all that remained was the horror of sinking down and down into the sinister depths.

He had cursed when his turn had come to guard the dam, but his secret dread was not something he could explain to such a man as Boss King. Why, he'd be laughed out of the outfit!

Now some sixth sense told him something was wrong. Straining his eyes he looked back along the wall that held back the Circle-Star's reservoir. His eyes must be playing him tricks, but he was sure he could see a tiny spark flickering close to the waterline. It was probably nothing, maybe some bug glowing in the dark, but deep down he knew there was no bug that sparked like that.

He began to edge along the dam, conscious of the drop on one side and the evil, lapping water on the other. It was only when he was a quarter of the way out that he realised what it was that had attracted his attention. A mine had been attached to the dam.

For a brief moment, Curtis forgot his fear. He sprang forward and, reaching the point above the floating casks, gazed down at the fuse.

It was at that moment that Jason Shepherd, now wading waist deep, turned and saw the figure of Curtis crouching down on the dam. He swung up his gun and fired.

"Get him," he yelled to Frankie. "Kill the son of a

bitch before he puts the fuse out."

Frankie turned and raised his gun. Bullets whipped round Curtis, chipping splinters off the dam, but he did not raise the Remington he held in his hand. The flickering spark seemed to hypnotise him. Slowly he began to reach down – and at that moment the moonlight gleaming on the wavelets caused his terror to surge back. He knew he could not reach down in case he slipped into those dark depths waiting to claim him. This terror was more real than the fuse or the bullets. Luckily for him he was a poor target in the moonlight and almost out of range of the pistols.

Clinging desperately to the board walk with one hand, he cast off the hook and line that moored the raft then holding his rifle by the barrel, he placed the butt against it and pushed it from the dam as hard as he could. Slowly the floating mine drifted away.

Curtis watched it for a moment, and then became aware of the bullets. He raised his rifle and began firing back at the flashes that stabbed the darkness.

The shots had aroused other Circle-Star men. There was a boom as a Sharps crashed across the artificial lake, then more guns began to bark in counterpoint.

Curtis kept pumping bullets in the direction of the attackers. He was rewarded by hearing a sudden yelp of pain. While he fired he moved cautiously along the top of the dam, aware that any moment the mine was likely to explode.

Close to the bank Jason put his arm round the sagging form of Frankie, trying to drag him to dry land. A slim silver fountain suddenly sushed upwards in the moonlight as the heavy Sharps got closer to the target. The leader of the Silver Bend Cattlemen's Protection Association cursed soundlessly, his mind aflame with anger and disappointment. The raft had been cast off, that shadow on the dam had undone all his work. In rage he

131

fired his last shot at the creeping form of Curtis, then he pulled his arm away from Frankie as he realised he was dead.

At that second the spark reached the gun cotton. There was an explosion that echoed and re-echoed in the valley and an enormous tongue of orange flame sprang from the surface of the water. The blast struck Curtis like a giant hand and hurled him off the dam. His last thought before his world exploded into blackness was that he was being flung off the *right* side of the dam – he had escaped the terrible depths.

CHAPTER 13

Night pressed heavily on Silver Bend. In the marshal's office the two prisoners dozed fitfully, while in the dim yellow light of a small oil lamp Marshal Dolan sprawled back in his chair with his feet on the table, contemplating the half empty bottle of Old Vermont before him. He felt sad and tired yet sleep eluded him. Once he half roused when he heard a distant drumming of hooves, but when he was in this lethargic state he lost all curiosity. It never crossed his mind to wonder what this sound of horses by night could mean.

He took a liberal drink and at last his head began to nod. Soon unmusical snores indicated that the guardian of the peace of Silver Bend had found refuge in uneasy slumber.

It was the crash of the door being kicked open that jerked him to bleary wakefulness. Four men entered his office, led by a tall, red-haired fellow with a coiled rope in his hands.

"I want the key of that cell, Marshal," demanded Hyatt.

At his words Royle and Sam Cash sat up on their beds, rubbing their faces with their hands.

"What's all this?" Sam Cash asked.

"You'll know plenty soon enough," retorted one of the men.

"We've come as vigilantes to make sure justice is done proper," Hyatt explained. "Come on, Dolan, gimme the key."

"Looks like a lynchin' party to me, Sam," remarked Royle. "Waal, they'll have to get both of us."

"That ain't such a bad idea," said Hyatt. "I reckon

_"

"Git outa my office," said Marshal Dolan, suddenly standing up. "You ain't no right here, an' as long as I'm Marshal of Silver Bend there'll be no illegal neck-tie parties."

Hyatt laughed. "You ain't no marshal. From what I hear tell you resigned just afore Boss King wanted you to go an' arrest Royle at the Good Luck. An' seein' the hoss soldiers have pulled outa town, why me an' the boys are the self-elected officers of law an' order – Ain't that so boys?"

There was muttered agreement.

"What's that about the hoss soldiers?" asked Dolan hoarsely.

"Why, they just rode outa town. There's been trouble out at the Circle-Star. I guess they won't be back until mornin'. They'll be a bit late then."

Suddenly a voice sounded from outside: "Hurry up an' bring that Circle-Star varmint out –we ain't gonna wait here all night..."

"There's quite a few citizens waitin' to give you a good send off, Cash," said Hyatt. "Okay, boys, we've wasted enough time. Get the key if the old buzzard won't hand over."

One of the men wrenched open the drawer under Dolan's table and took out a key.

"Here y'are," he said and advanced to the door of the cell.

"Goshdarn it, stop," said the marshal weakly, but the intruders ignored him.

Hyatt took the key and fitted it into the heavy lock.

"You oughta oil your locks, Dolan," he complained.

Next moment something arced through the air, something that gleamed briefly in the lamplight. It passed neatly through the bars and was caught by Lee Royle.

Marshal Dolan had thrown him his Colt Frontier.

Immediately Royle rammed the barrel through the bars into the soft belly of the bulky man bending over the lock.

"Don't move an inch," he hissed. "Marshal, come an' take the key off him. An' if any of you guys get any notions of gunplay, Hyatt here will be the first to get a taste of lead."

"Tell 'em, Hyatt, to drop their irons," said Sam Cash.

Sweat glistened amongst the red stubble on the big man's cheeks.

"Tell 'em, Hyatt," snapped Royle, prodding the shaking stomach viciously.

"Put 'em down boys," muttered Hyatt in the voice of a man who is face to face with his own fear and defeat. "Put 'em down for Gawd's sake."

Reluctantly the men placed their guns on the floorboards. They felt a keen sense of resentment, not against Royle but Hyatt. From a bullying leader, he had shrunk to a bungling coward.

"Now, git outa my office," said Dolan. "An' tell your pals to *vamos*. They'll be no lynchin' in Silver Bend."

"You're a durned fool, Marshal," said one of the men as he turned. "Now Royle has a gun they'll both bust outa jail."

Dolan ignored the remark. He walked over to the trembling Hyatt and chained his wrists to the cell bars with a pair of handcuffs.

"You'll be stayin' here the night," he said, "as a hostage."

When the men had gone, slamming the door behind them, Cash drew a deep breath. "Thanks, Marshal," he said. "I sure thought I was gonna get a rope collar."

135

"It was a pretty throw, Marshal," Royle added. "You got that six-gun damned neatly between them bars."

Dolan sat down and rewarded himself with a drink.

"I wasn't always the fella I am now," he said reflectively. "Life has a way of lousin' you up. But I'm still enough of the guy I was to give you a chance against that loudmouthed bum..."

"I guess you are at that," agreed Royle. He looked down at the Frontier in his hand.

"Er – Marshal, I guess you'd better take this pistol before it gives Sam an' me bad ideas." Sam nodded in agreement as Royle, holding the barrel, held the gun out between the bars.

For once Dolan's face actually smiled – slightly. "I was hopin' you'd do that, boy," he said, taking the Frontier. "I guess there's some that would have tried to bust out once they got a gun, but you've played it square." He put the pistol away, remarking: " 'Course I took the precaution of takin' the shells out when I first took it off you."

* * *

The cavalry returned at dawn, tired and ill-tempered. They had ridden out to the Circle-Star to prevent what reports had said was a large scale battle. When they had arrived they found that a home-made gun cotton mine had been exploded, but thanks to a guard on the dam it had drifted too far away from the structure to do much damage. The guard had been blown over the edge of the dam with the blast, and had been laid out with concussion. The only other sign of the night attack was a body of one of the raiders floating close to the bank.

In the Silver Lode Captain Powers was in a temper. He hated this job, hated Silver Bend, and above all he hated the men he was here to stop from murdering each other. How he wished that a telegram from the Silver Bend Cattlemen's Protection Association had never been dispatched to Congress, warning that a range war was brewing. If it had not been for that, the locals would have been left free to blaze away as much as they liked and Captain Powers and his troopers would have been left alone for their proper duties. This peacekeeping was no job for a crack corps.

There was something about the locals Captain Powers despised, the way they slouched, the unmilitary way they wore their guns and the sneaking way they fought – a shot here, an assassination there, a raid that ended up as a fiasco. It was all so unprofessional.

In his room the captain was pouring himself out a ration of rum when the door flew open and a trooper, in what appeared to be a white uniform, reeled in. Captain Powers started up, and realised that the man's uniform had become white with trail dust. He was staggering with fatigue.

"I've got a dispatch for you, Captain," he said, managing to make a passable salute. "I've come full gallop from Carsonville with it. It came through the telegraph."

"At ease, trooper," said Powers, taking the envelope. Then he proffered the glass of rum to the courier. The trooper's dust-caked mask broke into a smile, but it snapped back into regulation blankness when the captain added acidly: "And for God's sake, do up your tunic button. You are a soldier not a goddam cowboy."

As he read the paper a glow began to grow in the captain's heart. He relaxed his own iron self-discipline enough to even smile at the messenger. "Get out and send me the bugler. Howling Wolf's put on the paint and left his reservation with five hundred braves. We've got an Indian war on our hands, boy, and we're pulling out of this goddamned shanty town."

As the bugle call rang through the early morning air, and the tired men cursed as they threw back their blankets after just getting into them, there was stern joy in the captain's heart. War, real war, with an enemy that understood war perhaps better than any other race, lay ahead. There would be campaigns and ambushes, sudden charges over rolling plains and pitched battles in remote valleys. The captain put his fingers up to his black patch, the patch he had worn ever since a Sioux arrow had taken his eye, and then went out to address his men.

Just before the troops rode out of Silver Bend, Captain Powers went to the marshal's office. He ignored the two grinning prisoners, and the large, red-haired man who sat uncomfortably on the floor with his wrists chained, and said to Dolan: "Marshal, I have to take my men away for a far more important job than keeping order in Silver Bend. Therefore, the protection of life an' property in this town is once again your responsibility. Do you understand –"

The last question was because Dolan was looking up at him from his chair with blank eyes and stupid grin on his face. "Anythin' you shay, sojer," muttered Dolan. "The Yankees ish leavin' – hurrah! The Shouth shall rish again!"

"You're wastin' your words, general," said Cash cheerfully. "The old devil's been celebratin'."

Without a word Captain Powers turned on his heel and walked into the bright morning where his men were lined up on their mounts as though on parade.

Reluctantly he gave orders for two troopers to remain to guard the prisoners, then the cavalcade jingled down Main Street to vanish into a cloud of trail dust.

* * *

Trooper Jim Wilson looked at the fan of cards in his hand and could not believe his luck. A Royal Flush! A real, genuine, one-hundred per cent Royal Flush, and the very first one he had had in his life. But he did not allow his excitement to alter his deadpan features. So far he had

138

lost twenty dollars to the prisoners. Here was his chance for revenge.

He and his companions were sitting opposite Royle and Sam Cash. They had moved the marshal's table right up against the door of the cell, and had been playing poker through the bars. The marshal was nowhere to be seen. Having grumbled about Yankees interfering with his job, he had mooched off to nurse his hangover.

It was now a little after sunset, and the game had been getting more and more tense as the stakes rose. Royle looked up from his cards and smiled at the two young troopers.

"If I were you boys, I'd lay my cards down and elevate my hands," he said. "I say that 'cause you're nice fellas, an' it would be a pity for such a pleasant game to end badly." At his words Sam Cash looked up.

"Goddarn it, *compadres*" he grinned. "He's right. The drop is on you."

Not quite comprehending, the two troopers turned in their chairs. By the door stood a dark figure, gun in hand. It had a dark hat pulled well down over its eyes and a kerchief covered the lower half of its face. A dark poncho hung down from its shoulders and in the feeble light of the lamp it was hard to make out any details.

A movement of the gun barrel told the troopers to get to their feet and stand to one side. They obeyed, holding their hands at shoulder height.

"Looks like help is at hand," said Sam Cash. Royle put his hands through the bars and disarmed the men quickly. "Let's have the cell key, Jim," he said.

Jim Wilson took out the key and unlocked the cell door.

"It just ain't fair," he cried.

"What ain't?" asked Royle. "It can't worry you none that we gonna go free..."

"It ain't that – I had a Royal Flush in my hand."

Royle turned over the cards.

"Glory!" he exclaimed. "Take a look at that, Sam."

Sam whistled. The figure at the door waved its gun impatiently.

"Better get inside, fellas," said Royle. "Sorry about that Flush."

When the two soldiers were imprisoned in the cell, Royle and Sam Cash followed their silent rescuer into the deserted street, buckling on their guns. Outside Royle paused, swung out the cylinder of his Frontier and began pushing cartridges into the empty chambers.

"Quick, I have a spare horse. You must ride behind me, Lee." At these words Royle nearly dropped his revolver while Sam Cash's mouth sagged open.

"Miss Quinn?" he gasped.

"The same," she said. "But we haven't got time to discuss that now. Follow me, there's trouble headin' this way."

Wordlessly they followed her to a hitching rail where two horses were tied.

"You take the roan, Sam," she said. "Head back to the Circle-Star. You may meet a posse of riders comin' in to Silver Bend .. ."

"What's it all about, Miss?"

"Since they tried to blow up the dam last night Dad has gone to war in earnest on the settlers and small ranchers. When the word got through that the cavalry had pulled out, Slim got a bunch together and they're headin' this way to spring you from jail..."

"If they're gonna do that, why did you bother, Miss King, much as I 'preciate it?"

"Because they also planned to hang Mister Royle."

"There's a lot of people with hangin' on the mind," said Sam Cash. "Okay, Miss I understand. I'll head back to the ranch. Keep your powder dry, Royle, you may be needin' it."

140

"Be seein' ya, Sam," replied Royle.

"*Hasta la vista*," and the bearded gunman galloped down the street.

"Get up behind me," ordered Ella Quinn. Royle climbed up as he was bid and at a touch of Ella's quirt the horse cantered away from Marshal Dolan's office.

"Where we goin', Ella?" Royle asked, but she shook her head to discourage conversation.

Soon they were riding along a little-used trail whose dusty surface caught just enough light to look like a vague pale ribbon curving ahead through the dry sagebrush.

An hour went by, and now there was enough moonlight for Royle to make out the bulk of The Plateau to the north. Obviously Ella had skirted the usual trail to avoid meeting the Circle-Star party.

Once Royle tried to express his thanks, but she did not reply.

At length she reined up by a large white rock that reared up from the plain like some strange idol of a forgotten age.

Royle slipped down to rest the horse, but Ella remained in the saddle. She was wearing range-riding clothes like a man, but she had shaken her hair loose from under her dark Stetson, and Royle drew in his breath as he saw the beautiful profile of her face against the moonlit rock.

"I hardly know how to thank you," said Royle. "You took a mighty big risk for me..."

"Don't thank me. You did the same for me when the prairie was afire. Now we're even." She spoke harshly, and Royle looked up to her face to try and fathom what troubled her.

"I'm mighty worried in case you get into trouble with your father over what you've done," he said.

"Don't you worry about that, Mister Royle. I am

141

not goin' back to the Circle-Star. My father's like a crazy man since they tried to blow up his dam. He sent his men out to cut fences and burn barns, and to shoot-to-kill settlers who tried to stop him. I can't stand him like that. Maybe that dam has come to mean more to him than he knows, maybe it's become some sort of obsession. But whatever the reason, he's out for blood as much as any of his hired gunslingers. I don't know him any more. He was always hard, but now."

"What are you gonna do, Ella?"

"I'm going to head south, to Tucson. My mother lives down there. When I was a child I could never understand why she left Dad. I never forgave her. I guess she just knew him better than me."

There was silence for a while.

"If you head south-west you'll reach your brother's place, Mister Royle," said Ella coldly.

"Ella, why are you talkin' this way? When we was in Skull Canyon – remember – you – "

"I remember all right, Mister Royle. I remember what you said – do you?"

"Yes, I do, Ella. I guess I kinda said I loved you – that I'd like to settle down – "

Ella laughed bitterly.

"Sure you did. At the time it made me very happy to hear it. It's a pity you hadn't the courage to tell me the truth –"

"What is the truth then?"

"On the day you shot Pete Montana and the Circle-Star sieged the Good Luck Saloon, my father ordered me back home. Well for once I didn't do what he told me. We'd had a difference of opinion about this water war, so I rode out to your brother's place. I don't really know why. I wanted to see your sister-in-law, I guess. Maybe I hoped I could talk to Ethan and get him to try an' stop the fightin'. I did not realise he's been wounded so bad.

142

Anyway, I talked to Linda, an' Linda told me all about you, Lee Royle. She told me the things you'd forgotten to tell in Skull Canyon."

Royle bit his lips. As he looked up at her face, framed in her blue-black hair and her eyes large and mysterious in the shadows, he felt a sad longing in his heart. It was a longing for something he knew he was losing.

"Go on," he said softly. "What did Linda tell you?"

"That you have been to jail for murder, and that you are married."

Royle sighed. He suddenly felt old and tired – he had no strength to argue.

"Have you anything to say to that, Mister Royle?"

He shook his head.

Ella's horse began to move restlessly. Automatically she patted its neck. Then Royle said: "If you feel disappointed at what you heard, why did you bother to get me outa jail?"

"Because I owed you a debt, an' we Quinns always pay up. I've paid you back for the fire, now I want to square it up over Skull Canyon."

Her arm suddenly swung close to Royle. Her quirt caught him savagely across the face, slicing open the flesh over his left cheekbone. The wound was agonising, but he remained motionless and silent, not even putting his hand up to stop the blood that was flowing freely down his face.

"Remember me by that," hissed Ella, suddenly pale at the sight of the blood which appeared black in the moonlight. "An' if it's any satisfaction to you, I'll remember you by an aching heart."

She wheeled her horse and touched its flank with the whip which was wet with Royle's blood. He watched as she galloped back down the trail, then he turned and began to walk in the direction of his brother's home, pressing his bandana against the throbbing gash.

143

CHAPTER 14

"Lee, what's happened to you?" cried Linda as her brother-in-law walked into the kitchen, the side of his face stained with dried blood.

"I had an accident after I got outa jail," he replied. "How's Ethan?"

"A lot better. We've been worried sick over you. We heard how you'd been jailed by that army captain, an' how someone tried to blow up the Circle-Star dam. What's going to happen, Lee?"

"I don't know, an' I don't care. I'm quittin'. I did what I came to do. Now I'm hittin' the trail again."

In the east the sun had just risen above the horizon, and a wave of heat was rolling across the plain. From Linda's stove came the smell of coffee, but Royle ignored it.

"Linda, before I go, I wanna ask you somethin'."

"Yes?" She looked apprehensive.

"Why did you tell Ella Quinn what you did?"

She turned away from him, busying herself with the coffee.

"She asked me about you. I just told her the truth."

"Goddam it, Linda, there's many brands of truth."

"I told her the truth. I told her you'd been wed, an' I told her you'd been jailed. It's true, ain't it' – you can't deny it!"

"No I can't, but did you tell her why – did you tell her how my wife had run off before I met you? Did you tell her how she went back East with that fella? Did you tell her how she died of childbirth a couple of years later in Boston? An' did you tell her why I was jailed as a murderer? Goddam it, it wasn't murder. The man I killed was rustlin' our steers, an' I was the only one who tried to stop him. My Dad was too old, an' Ethan' – well, Ethan – but I went after him to get our cattle back, an' it was him or me. He died in a fair fight, the only thing was I hadn't any witnesses. The rustlin' gang not only had witnesses, they had a lawyer. I was lucky I didn't swing, an' yet I'd only been protectin' what was rightful property. Did you tell Ella that?"

Linda said nothing.

"Why did you tell her the so-called truth about me? Why did you wanna bust us up?"

Linda turned on him, her face suddenly drawn.

"Because I didn't want her to get you, Lee. Before you went to jail you used to love me."

"Waal, maybe you should have waited," said Royle sardonically.

"Life ain't like that, Royle. I couldn't face all those years stretching ahead. Why, I'd have been an old woman when you came out. How was I to know you'd get pardoned? So I married Ethan – he was like you, but he was kind too – I've been happy with him, but' – but, God forgive me, I still love you –"

"No, you don't," Royle hissed. "If you loved me, you'd have wanted me to be happy, to get somethin' out of life that I missed so far – what you got for me ain't love, Linda. You want everythin'" – the life Ethan has given you' – an' me. You couldn't bear to see me marry another woman. Maybe you even wanted to pay me back for getting put in jail an' leavin' you – waal, if it's any consolation, Linda, you've won. I've lost Ella, an' now I'm hittin' the trail."

Linda threw her arms round him, pulling his face down to hers so that some of Royle's blood rubbed off on her cheek. He tried to push her away, but she clung to him and cried: "You mustn't go – I love you."

Suddenly her arms went loose and dropped to her

side. She was looking past Royle with an expression of fear on her face. Slowly he turned and saw Ethan, gaunt-faced, in the doorway.

There was a silence that seemed to last for an eternity. Then Ethan said weakly: "Lee, I cannot find it in my heart to hate any man, but you must leave my home – "

"I was goin' anyways," Royle said. "Now the well is dug –"

Linda laughed hysterically. "The well – the well – your well ain't no more, Lee, an' I'm glad' – do you under-stand' – I'm glad they came an' blowed it up – "

Royle swung round on her.

"What are you talkin' about, woman?"

"The Circle-Star! Some of their men came yesterday. I saw them through the window. They dropped something down the well and rode off – and a minute later there was a great explosion, and now the well is all filled in."

"You mean they blasted my well?" demanded Royle in a thick voice, turning back to Ethan. He nodded, clutching the edge of the door for support.

Lee felt in his pocket, drawing the silver dollars out of his pocket that he had won from Trooper Wilson the night before.

"That's for your horse, Ethan," he said. "I got business back in Silver Bend." As he walked out of the door he kept muttering to himself, "They never oughta blowed up my well – "

* * *

"I'm right with you all the way, Jason," said Royle.

"Last time we spoke you said you weren't on no-one's side," said the heavily bearded leader of the Silver Bend Cattlemen's Protection Association. "Somethin' make you change your mind?"

"Yeah, the sons of bitches blew up my well."

"It figures," said Jason Shepherd. "All yesterday Boss Quinn had his men on the warpath. They burned several homes, an' several guys ended up with lead poisonin'. Anyways, Royle, I'm durned glad to have you with us. We been workin' out a plan of attack –"

Royle looked at the half dozen men sitting in the smoke-filled room.

Down below at least sixty men were in the bullet-scarred saloon, waiting for Jason Shepherd to give the orders to ride out to the Circle-Star.

"Boss Quinn had it his way when we were all scattered about," he said, "but now we've got together we outnumber him. The tables are sure gonna be turned today."

"It's gonna be tough," Royle said. "I been out to the Circle-Star ranch. It's built to stand a siege, there's even iron shutters they can close over the windows with rifle slits in them. The trouble is they can cover the dam from the ranch house."

"I know. We'll have to pin them down while a party gets up to the dam with explosive. This time there ain't gonna be any chance of it driftin' away."

"What we need is a field gun," muttered Royle. "There's some durn good shots in that bunch –"

Jason Shepherd grinned. "You come down with me," he said. He led Royle and his lieutenants down the stairs to the back of the saloon.

"Goddamn," exclaimed Royle. "Where in tarnation did you get that?"

"It was left over from the war," Jason Shepherd explained.

The object which caused the surprise was a cannon that had been mounted on a light cart.

"Tell him about it, Otis," said one of the men. A wiry little settler in his fifties, who had been working on

147

the gun, straightened up.

"I was an artillery man in the war," he said with a touch of pride. "When the surrender took place I was durned if I was gonna let the Yankees have my Betsy –" he indicated the cannon. "I stripped it off the carriage, an' took it back to my place in an old wagon. For years I had it under straw in my barn, an' then when I came to settle in this part of the country I couldn't leave old Betsy behind, so along she came in my waggon."

"Will it fire?" asked Royle.

"Don't rightly know," said Otis. "She ain't been fired for years, but she's a simple old muzzle loader an' I don't see why not. I ain't got no shot for her, of course, but we got some lumps of metal an' canisters from the blacksmith's. I been workin' in secret on Betsy for some time now."

"I want you to take charge of Betsy," said Jason to Royle. "Otis'll fire it, but I want you to get it to the right spot. Come back inside an' I'll draw you a map."

Within an hour the Silver Bend 'army' set out, cantering along the trail that led towards The Plateau. Royle, Otis and six others rode in a westerly direction. Jason's plan was to get the gun up to the top of the western cliffs overlooking the Circle-Star valley. Then, while the ancient artillery began to bombard the ranch, a party would take explosives to the eastern end of the dam.

Soon the main party was lost to sight.

"We're on our own now, old-timer," Royle said to Otis. "I hope you still know how to set it off."

"I could never forget how to lay a gun," chuckled Otis. "But I never thought I'd have a chance to do it again." He whipped up the horses pulling the light, two-wheeled cart. It bounced over the rough ground and the small party made good progress towards The Plateau.

Some time later the wind brought the faint echo of shots.

148

"Sounds like the enemy's engaged," remarked Otis. "C'mon, men, we got to get Betsy up to the top of that there sawn-off mountain."

By noon they were approaching the steep slopes that led up to the flat top of The Plateau.

As the going got harder, the horses, already whipped to a lather, began to flounder.

"All right, fellas," said Royle. "This is where we take over." The horses were hobbled, and the men began to manhandle the cart. Luckily Betsy was a light gun, but even so the sweat started from their skins as they heaved on the wheels and tugged the ropes that were attached to the axles.

Inch by inch they fought their way up the slope. Often it seemed the cart would career back downhill, and the men on the ropes had to cling to thorn bushes or the outcrops of jagged rocks while the wheel men heaved on the spokes until it jerked forward again.

As they climbed higher and higher Royle found the way got steeper. Looking up he wondered how they were going to get Betsy up the almost perpendicular slope.

Suddenly there was a shot. The man on the rope next to Royle coughed, clawed the air for a moment and went rolling down the incline.

The men threw themselves flat, trying to squirm behind cover without letting go the ropes which held Betsy from plunging after the victim of the sniper. Another bullet whistled down to hit a rock and ricochet away over the plain.

"Hang on," ordered Royle. He released his rope and scrambled down to the cart where he packed stones behind the wheels. Then he seized his Winchester which was in the cart. Bullets splintered the woodwork of the improvised gun carriage before he threw himself flat.

"Okay, she's safe now," he called. The men dropped the ropes and drew their pistols, squinting up at the edge of the bluff and the blue sky beyond. Of the Circle-Star man they could see no sign. Yet he was obviously in a good vantage point because the slightest movement of the pinned-down men was enough to bring bullets whistling about them.

Cautiously Royle began to inch up the slope. His eyes would pick out the next piece of cover, then he would dive forward and throw himself prone behind it. Each time he did this the man above fired. And on the last occasion Royle thought he saw a puff of smoke slightly to the left, on die rim of The Plateau. He swung the barrel of the Winchester round to the point. The seconds crawled by, then he caught a slight movement in the clump of thorn on which his sights rested. He fired. There was a thrashing movement in the bush and a figure reared up on the edge of the skyline, a hand clapped to his head. He was only poised there for seconds, but several six-shooters crashed behind Royle and a volley of Colt bullets caught the rifleman, spinning him out of sight.

A stillness followed the sudden burst of shooting. Was the Circle-Star man alone, or did he have a mate waiting at another vantage point for the men to stand up and start hauling Betsy again?

Royle took off his hat and slowly edged it from behind the rock where he was sheltering. No bullet plucked it from his hand.

"C'mon, boys," he called. "The war'll be over before we get Betsy to the top if we ain't careful. Jesse, go down an' see if there's anythin' we can do for Hank."

"All we can do is bury him later on," reported Jesse. "Poor crittur stopped it right in the pump."

Once more the ropes became taut and the men at the wheels heaved on the spokes.

When the gun was finally heaved over the lip of The Plateau, the men flung themselves flat and drew in air in great sobbing gasps. After a minute Royle sat up and looked about him. Not far away lay the huddled form of the sniper, a small cloud of evil flies already dancing over him.

Turning from the dismal sight, Royle surveyed the top of The Plateau. It was flat tableland of over a hundred square miles. In a forgotten age nature had pushed up a huge section of the plain, leaving its surface smooth apart from the great valleys that millions of years of rain had eroded through it.

Wearily the men climbed to their feet and grasped the ropes with raw hands, hauling in a direction that Otis indicated after squinting at a pocket compass. Apart from the stalks of dried out grass and the odd clump of dwarf oak, there was little vegetation and they were able to keep Betsy rolling at a good walking pace. Sometimes the sound of gunfire came faintly to their ears.

Half an hour later they arrived at the edge of the Circle-Star valley and gazed down. There was little to see. Occasionally gunsmoke appeared to drift from the ranch buildings, while a slight haze from certain points indicated the position of the attackers. Otis drew out a battered army telescope which he pulled to full length and began to sweep the valley.

"I guess our boys have got the Circle-Star bottled up, but likewise they can't risk a head-on attack. They'd be mown down on the flats round the ranch. It looks to me like there's some Circle-Star defence at the dam, too. Durned if I can see how Jason is gonna get his blastin' powder there."

"Let's give the Circle-Star somethin' to rile 'em up a bit, then," said Royle. "We ain't come here to admire the view."

"You bet," said Otis and began giving orders. Betsy was rolled into position at the edge of the valley wall and Otis squinted along the barrel.

"Reckon that'll do her," he said after he had made

a few adjustments. "Can only tell after we see how the first shot goes."

Grinning to himself he rammed home a charge of gunpowder, then some sacking as improvised wadding and finally a heavy metal weight. He lit a long fuse, and ordered the men to run for it. They obeyed with alacrity and threw themselves flat while the fuse smoked, and Otis watched the scene below through his telescope.

There was an ear-splitting explosion as the old gun vomited flame. The cart rocketed backwards with the recoil.

A column of dust floated up by the corner of Boss Quinn's ranch house.

"Not bad," muttered Otis. "Reckon we'll give them a canister this time."

"What's that?" asked Royle.

"Sorta home-made shell," Otis explained. "We used to make 'em when we was short of shot an' that was often enough. I been makin' 'em for the last week."

Betsy was wheeled back into position, and Otis reloaded. As he did so several bullets hummed over his head. Obviously the advent of artillery had not gone unnoticed by the defenders of the Circle-Star.

When the charge and wadding was pounded home, Otis produced a metal container from the ammunition box which was bolted to the cart. A long fuse dangled from it. This he lit before sliding it into the barrel. Then he ignited the touch-hole and ran for his life. Again Betsy spewed flame and this time threw herself on her side with the violence of her recoil. But the canister struck the wall of the ranch house and exploded, blasting a large hole and setting the shattered timbers ablaze. A faint cheer floated from down the valley.

"Dang it, Betsy, you ain't lost your knack, girl," cried Otis enthusiastically. "We'll blast them varmints to hell. Come on, let's get her into position again."

A hail of bullets swept from the ranch house. Several men lay on the roof and blazed away with the long distance Sharps buffalo guns. The fire was so intense that the gunners kept back from the edge while the cannon was reloaded. When all was ready they hastily rolled her into position, then ran back out of the line of fire. Only Otis seemed indifferent to the bullets. He gazed along the barrel for a long moment, then lit the fuse and ran. Sparks spurted from the touch hole and Betsy spoke for the third time. The shot hit the roof of the ranch house, sending up a geyser of flame. Royle saw several of the riflemen hurled aside like skittles.

In the valley Royle saw a small group of figures moving in crouched positions towards the dam along the dry bed of the Snowy River. As yet the defenders had not been able to see them, but soon they could come into full view.

"D'you reckon you could get a shot on the dam before our boys reach it from here?" asked Royle. "Otherwise they'll be picked off by the Circle-Star fellas guardin' it."

"It's a durn sight further," said Otis. "But I could try. I'll use an extra charge an' grape on 'em."

Once more Betsy was righted and loaded. Otis lit the fuse and the gunners scattered. The seconds went by and nothing happened.

"The danged fuse has gone out," muttered Otis. He raced towards the gun.

Next instant the ground trembled. In the explosion fragments of shattered cannon screamed through the air, cutting scars through the grass and whining into the heavens. When the choking powder smoke began to thin all that remained of Betsy was a length of twisted metal.

Royle bent over the blackened form of Otis.

Slowly the old gunner opened his eyes and shook his head. "The bitch," he muttered, "to think I looked after her all them years an' she does this to me."

"You hurt or anythin'?" inquired Royle.

"Don't think so," said Otis. He slowly climbed to his feet. Then he held out his hand, palm upwards like a child who expects a sweet.

"I can't believe it," he muttered.

"Can't believe what?" Royle asked.

It's rainin'!"

CHAPTER 15

Wraiths of vapour rose from the parched earth as the drizzle fell upon it. To the men attacking the Circle-Star it was a blessed relief, the coolness and moisture making them grin with pleasure as they looked along their gun barrels at the distant ranch buildings. When Royle and his men reached the valley after trying to shell the Circle-Star, Jason Shepherd told them the attempt to blow up the dam had failed.

"Two of the boys were shot to death, an' Matt was plugged bad but managed to get back," he said. "While you fellas had old Betsy firin' away, they went up the dry bed of Old Snowy. They had shelter from the banks for a lot of the way, then suddenly, when they was quite close, a guy stood up on the dam as cool as you please an' started blazin' away. He sure must be a mighty fine shot' – my boys didn't even have time to loose off a single slug before two had cashed their chips an' Matt was limpin' back with a great hole through his thigh."

"What happened to the explosive?" Royle asked.

"I guess it's by their bodies. I sent some more guys scoutin' off to try and kill this fella, but he managed to shoot one an' beat the others off. They reckon they ain't seen shootin' like it. While he holds the dam there's not a chance in hell of us blowin' it."

"Do you know who it is?" Royle inquired.

"Nope, not for certain, but my bet is it's Sam Cash."

"That's what I was thinkin'," Royle said reflectively. "Waal, Jason, let me handle this. We've got to blow that dam if it's the last durned thing we ever do. One guy alone can't hold us back for ever. An' Sam an' I gotta shoot it out, sooner or later. It's in the stars."

"I was hopin' you'd say that," said Jason. "I guess you're the only fella on our side who's been a professional slinger–"

The look on Royle's face hardened.

"I guess I have my uses," he muttered finally. "S'long, Jason."

Royle ran forward with his Winchester in one hand. For a while he followed the hard mud of the Snowy, but before he came within range of the dam or the distant ranch house, he climbed the east bank and began skirting through the stunted scrub.

As he made his way, he almost tripped over the prone figure of a man gazing over a double-barrelled rifle in the direction of the dam.

"Howdy," he said, turning his head at Royle's approach. "If you go further than this point you're in dead trouble' – in fact you're dead. Look down the slope, there's Jeff's body with a bullet through the head."

"How come?" said Royle, crouching down beside the settler.

"It's that fella on the dam," was the reply. "He's the best shot I've ever seen. He's down behind some beams they put up as a sorta barricade, right in the middle of the dam – See."

As he watched Royle saw a puff of smoke suddenly appear on the top of the dam. It was the only visible sign he was in a battle.

"Where are the first guys he shot?" asked Royle.

"You can't see 'em from here. I guess they must be about a hundred feet from the dam. They thought the banks would protect them from the ranch buildings, but they didn't figure this hombre would be waitin' for 'em. He hadn't fired a shot until then."

"I'd 'preciate it if you'd give him some rapid fire. I know the distance is too great to do much damage, but it'll

156

give him somethin' to think on while I try an' get close."

"Okay, pal," said the settler, pressing his cheek against the stock. "Sooner you than me."

As the first shot crashed, Royle began moving through the fringe of scrub. He thought he had seen a tine of cover that ran down to the east end of the dam. But first he had to reach it, and this meant a wide detour through the scrub. As he ran doubled up he heard the regular report of the double-barrelled rifle, but there was no answering fire. The man on the dam seemed as though he was not interested in wasting ammunition on distant snipers.

The sweat trickled down Royle's face. By now the rain was increasing the humidity, and he felt as though he was in a bath house. He also felt very tired – the jailbreak, the parting with Ella, the long trek to his brother's place the night before, the strain of getting Betsy to the top of The Plateau, and now the tension of the battle were almost too much for his endurance. His limbs felt leaden, and several times he stopped, threw himself flat and panted for air.

At last he reached what he was hoping to find. The line he had glimpsed from the settler's firing position turned out to be a narrow natural ditch which drained water into the Snowy in normal times.

Royle tore up a withered bush, threw it into the narrow runnel and, laying flat behind it, began squirming slowly along. Soon he was out of the protection of the scrub, and he knew that if he were to rise from a prone position he would be immediately in line of fire from the dam. Cautiously he inched his way along, moving his camouflage ahead and pulling his rifle along by the barrel. The bottom of the ditch had already started to collect rain, and little by little the rock-hard clay was turning to mud, making the going slippery.

As minutes crawled, Royle's attention was focused

solely on the journey along the old watercourse. The sounds of shooting, even the knowledge that soon he would confront Sam Cash and that the death of one or the other might only be minutes away, receded. His concentration was taken up completely by his uncomfortable journey.

Suddenly he froze, a cry of horror stillborn in his throat. A couple of yards ahead, in the shadow of the bank, he saw the unmistakable markings of a rattlesnake. For what seemed an eternity he lay paralysed while he fought to gain control of himself. He knew that any movement might cause the reptile to rear and swing its lethal head at his face. Yet if he tried to get out of its way a bullet would probably accomplish what the hollow fangs failed. He just lay, waiting for inspiration that did not come. No doubt the rain had wakened the snake from a sun-drugged sleep, probably it was still drowsy. Perhaps he could risk a slight movement.

Slowly Royle drew back his right hand, the sweat breaking out afresh when a clump of dead reeds trembled as he touched them. Slowly he twisted his elbow, and slowly his hand moved down to his holster. He figured that he had more chance of drawing his Colt than bringing up the rifle. There was an instinctive feeling of relief as his fingers closed on the damp butt of the Frontier. Now came the difficult part, drawing the gun up and getting it into position.

As Royle kept his eyes fastened on the form of the snake he could have sworn that it was beginning to undulate. He mastered an urge to bring up the Colt quickly and blaze away at the hateful coils. But he knew that fast as he was on the draw, he could never beat the speed of a striking rattler.

At last the gun was level with his head, then he was raising it slowly, ever so slowly, at arm's length. He got his sights on the place where he thought the head should

158

be, but the sweat was running into his eyes which kept going out of focus with the strain.

He lowered his head and blinked rapidly to clear his vision, then once more he raised the gun and began to squeeze the trigger. He knew that the shot might give his position away to the guardian of the dam, but that was a risk he had to take. The pressure increased, but before the hammer could fall, Royle lowered the gun and began to choke with the hysterical laughter of relief. Droplets from a flurry of rain suddenly sparkled all over the snake as they were caught in the spiders' webs that were woven about it. Certainly no living snake would be cobwebbed, the rattler which had turned Royle's blood to ice was merely the cast-off skin of a snake which had probably lain in the ditch for weeks or even months.

Sighing with relief, Royle began to move forward again, though when he crawled past the scaly skin he could not help shuddering, not at the thing as it was but for what he had thought it had been.

Minutes later he found the walls of the bank becoming lower and lower as the ditch widened out. It was here that the water carried by the ditch flowed into the Snowy. Raising his head above the bank, now only about a foot high, Royle saw he was close to the end of the dam. There was no sign of its defender. No doubt he was still on the centre wall, ensconced behind his beams.

Royle knew if he could climb the earth works he might be able to fire along the top of the dam. It would mean a swift scramble,, and he decided to leave the Winchester behind. Subconsciously he was glad of this decision as he always felt happier with a Colt. He got to his knees and within seconds was flat against the sloping earthwork. Being on the eastern side of the dam he was not visible from the ranch buildings, while as long as he remained close to the side of the dam he was out of his enemy's angle of vision.

For some moments he lay against the dam, breathing deeply and steeling himself for the rush. The rain had increased and now fell in curtains across the valley, cutting down visibility.

"Well, Sam," Royle murmured to himself. "Here I come, *compadre*."

He scrabbled up the slippery slope until his head was over the edge. Looking along the top of the curving dam, he could make out the shape of a man lying behind a balk of timber. He was not looking in Royle's direction, but was watching the bed of Old Snowy below him.

Carefully Royle raised the Frontier, extending it until the dark shape of the Circle-Star man and barrel were in a fateful line.

Until this moment the man on the dam had been an enemy, a factor that had to be eliminated in the more important work of destroying Boss Quinn's evil handiwork, but now treacherous memories flooded into Royle's mind – he remembered Sam Cash on the trail, Sam Cash deflecting his gun to Ulysses in the battle of Main Street, and the joking Sam Cash in Marshal Dolan's cell.

"Sam," yelled Royle. "I've come to get you."

At his words the figure moved convulsively, bringing a rifle to bear on Royle's head. The Colt and the rifle exploded together. A bullet nicked a piece of flesh out of Royle's neck just below his right ear. He ducked down, conscious of the warm blood running down the side of his neck, as yet not feeling any pain. He wondered if his bullet had struck Cash.

If he was unhurt, or slightly wounded, he would be waiting wolfishly for Royle's head to reappear.

The water was running down the earthworks, making it difficult for Royle to keep his position. After a moment's thought he relaxed his hold and allowed himself to slide down the muddy slope. Then, at the foot of the dam, he began to edge along the base. Soon he was knee deep in the water that gathered in pools from the jets that splashed from the cracks between the heavy pieces of wood. Some of these spurted over Royle as he continued his sideways journey.

By the time he was under the spot where he estimated Sam Cash to be, he was up to his waist. He knew that he was safe as long as he remained where he was. The man above would have to expose himself fatally before he could bring his rifle to bear on him.

With his pistol ready, Royle looked up at the edge of the dam about five feet above his head. The plank walk jutted out over him and it was on this, behind the protective timber, that Cash lay. Royle carefully looked at the chinks of light between the boards to gauge the exact position of his enemy. Then he took careful aim and fired.

A curse sounded from above. Next instant Royle saw the silhouette of a man against the sky. The defender of the dam was leaning over with his gun, pointing it directly at Royle. In the split second before Royle's finger tightened on his trigger, he became aware that drops of blood were falling on him with the rain. Then his Colt crashed. The rifle replied as though by reflex action, the bullet kicking up a stalk of water several yards away.

As he fired again the figure slowly toppled and plunged over the edge, splashing close to Royle. For a moment it was out of sight, then, as it surfaced, Royle found himself gazing down into the dead face of Slim Springfield.

* * *

Miles to the north of the Circle-Star valley the drought broke dramatically over Mount Snowy. The drizzle that had drifted down and cooled the men while they battled over Boss Quinn's dam was merely the edge of the rainstorm, in the centre the water fell from the sky in endless torrents. It was not rain but a cloudburst, and a cloudburst that continued through the day. Down the slopes of the mountain the water ran in a million trickles, trickles that were rejected by the drought-hardened earth so they flowed on to join other trickles. In turn these became rivulets on the lower slopes. It was as though the whole surface of the mountain was covered with a moving skin of water.

Before long the rivers that in normal times drained the mountain were beginning to swell. Soon they were past their pre-drought waterlines. The main course, the Snowy River, took most of the drainage. The rain had come so fast, and flowed so quickly down the slopes that had lost their vegetation and ability to absorb water, that a great head of yellow foaming water had built up and was roaring along its bed.

The flood was not the gradual rising that is experienced after prolonged rainfall, it was a sudden angry wall of water that swept between the banks with the dramatic appearance of a tidal wave.

When there is a drought two things happen to a river. Firstly it shrinks to a narrow ghost of its former self, and secondly, the mudflats that were once its bed become the only place where vegetation thrives in the stricken area. So, as the water began to flow down the Snowy, it was constantly checked by barriers of scrub. These would hold it briefly before the pressure increased and they were swept away with the current.

The debris would then be hurled on to the next patch and the process repeated so the river moved in a series of jerks, building up natural dams and wrecking them with equal violence.

As the water surged along the canyons and through the valleys of The Plateau, it was constantly fed by streams which had returned to life in forgotten watercourses.

By the time this great tumbling, roaring wall of

clay-coloured water approached the top of the long Circle-Star valley it was carrying with it a vast scum of writhing brushwood, among which lunged uprooted trees and the bodies of cattle swept away before they had time to reach higher ground. It was as though nature, tired of inflicting drought on the land, had suddenly decided to wreak a more terrible havoc by sending the rain.

The rain, however, still fell gently as Royle left the Circle-Star dam. Crouching low to avoid any bullets that might come his way from the ranch house, he made his way to the sprawled victims of the late Slim Springfield's marksmanship.

He was kneeling over the pack of explosive when Jason Shepherd and several of his men approached him through the drizzle.

"So you got Cash?"

Royle shook his head. "It wasn't Cash, it was Springfield," he explained.

Jason Shepherd's lips tightened in an expression of satisfaction.

"Good," he muttered. "I still have a chance to even things up for Ulysses myself. Say, there's blood runnin' down your neck –"

"I know," winced Royle. "Bind it up, will you?"

After the blood had been stopped, the small party made its way back to the dam. Here Jason began to place the charges and cut the fuse into suitable lengths with his sheath knife.

Meanwhile, on the floor of the valley, the settlers who circled the ranch buildings kept up a continuous fire to prevent any Circle-Star diehards from making a dash to save the dam. There was little chance of them making such a desperate gesture. Outnumbered and surrounded, they were pinned down by the hail of bullets that flattened themselves against the timbered walls. They contented themselves by firing back at the tell-tale puffs of smoke through the rifle slits. For a while they were not even aware that Slim Springfield, who had been taking his turn at sentry go when the attack was launched, had fallen to Royle's Frontier.

"That should do it," said Shepherd with cold satisfaction when all the charges were ready.

"I'm gonna light the fuses now. Hightail it to the higher ground, nothin'll stand a chance that's in the way of the water once the dam goes."

The men did not need a second warning. They melted away into the scrub while Royle and Shepherd cursed their damp matches. After several attempts one sprang into flame, burning Shepherd's cupped hands. Seconds later the fuses were hissing.

"What's that noise?" asked Royle, cocking his head.

"Durned if I know, an' I guess this ain't the time to try and figure it out," replied Jason Shepherd.

At first the noise was a strange murmur which gradually grew to evil thunder. Low-pitched and menacing, it filled the valley, and as Royle began to follow Jason to safety he was sure the ground beneath his feet trembled.

As he gained the top of the bank, he heard Jason cry out: "Gawd A-mighty, look at that."

He was pointing through the brittle branches of the brushwood which covered the banks of the river's old course. Royle's eyes followed his outstretched arm and saw beyond the dam, right across the man-made lake that stretched up the Circle-Star valley, a line of foaming water. The giant wave was bearing down on the dam.

As he watched Royle could not help thinking how ironical it was men had died in attempts to destroy the dam, and now it was likely to be destroyed by natural forces anyway.

The wall of water hit the dam with an impact that

164

made it shake as though in an earthquake. A dirty wave reared up and gushed over the top, extinguishing the fuses and racing on down the bed of the river. It carried off the body of Slim Springfield and his victims with it.

The sluice gates were smashed, and a gash appeared in the top of the dam where a giant tree trunk had been hurled against it with the force of a battering ram. But Boss Quinn had built his dam well, it shuddered and groaned yet it survived the first shock of the roaring flood. Now water spilled over its top and cascaded through its broken sluices, but the dam remained the barrier Boss Quinn had intended it to be. The result was that almost before the eyes of the two watchers, the margins of the Circle-Star reservoir began to expand as every minute thousands of gallons surged into the valley.

Jason Shepherd began to laugh. He doubled up, purple in the face, gasping for air, and still his wild mirth exploded from him.

"Can't say I see it as that much of a joke," commented Royle laconically.

"Can't you see –" gasped Jason Shepherd. "Can't you see what's happenin'? The water's risin' – waal, soon it'll be floodin' round the Circle-Star ranch house. Quinn'll be washed out, thanks to his own dam!"

CHAPTER 16

Rain streaked through the night. The first violence of the downpour which had burst over Mount Snowy abated, but enough still fell to ensure the level of the water in the Circle-Star valley rose hour by hour.

Before dark Jason Shepherd had sent some of his men back to Silver Bend to fetch waterproofs, food and above all a supply of rum. Through the night the members of the Silver Bend Cattlemen's Protection Association huddled on the higher ground, a rifle shot from the ranch house, and cursed the rain with the same fluency as they had cursed the drought. Within hours the whole situation had changed. Now they muttered to each other about the danger of floods on the plain.

But this was unlikely. The network of streams would distribute the waters once they left The Plateau. The flood in the valley was a freak result of Boss Quinn's dam.

Once the clouds parted briefly, and in the faint moonlight the distant shape of the ranch house could be discerned surrounded by the black water.

"Reckon they'll be on the roof by mornin'," laughed one of the men between chattering teeth. "Pickin' 'em off will be easier'n shootin' crows."

As dawn came someone managed to make coffee on a little oil stove, and the warm drink laced with rum put new life into the bedraggled besiegers. As the rays of the sun struggled through the misty curtain hanging over The Plateau, the guns of Shepherd's men began to boom in unison. Bullets fountained into the water now almost up to the window frames of the ugly building.

A few half-hearted shots were fired in reply, but

these soon died away.

"Reckon the fight's gone outa 'em," Royle muttered to Jason Shepherd. "If they keep fightin' it'll be for only one reason' – the cussedness of Boss Quinn."

"Keep firin' boys," Jason shouted to his men. "Don't let the varmints think the war's over 'cause there's been a bit of rain."

Minutes later the door at the back of the house opened and a figure appeared waving a white cloth with an enthusiasm denoting his interest in survival.

The settlers lowered their guns and watched in silence as the man waded towards them. When he left the doorway he was up to his waist, and as he floundered forward the current eddied round him viciously. He was exhausted when he dragged himself wearily on to the higher ground.

"Mornin' Curtis," Jason Shepherd said laconically. "You look sorta damp."

Curtis, to whom the nightmare of wading through the flood was only slightly less terrifying than remaining in the ranch house and watching it creep up the walls, ignored him and handed his Smith & Wesson to Royle, butt first as a token of surrender.

"We've sure had a bellyful," he said. "The fellas wanna throw their hand in, but they don't wanna be mowed down if they come outa there unarmed."

"Go back an' tell 'em they can come out," said Jason Shepherd. "We'll take 'em back into Silver Bend an' they can stand trial for the murder of Luke Muldoon, Eddy, Ulysses an' all the others when that judge comes. Mebbe you should tell Sam Cash to come out with his Colt though, I gotta settle somethin' with him personal."

"He ain't there," said Curtis.

"What's happened to him?" asked Royle.

"He an' Boss Quinn quit durin' the night. It was Boss Quinn's idea to get clear an' then go to the State

Governor for help."

"D'ya know how he went?"

"I'm not certain sure, but I figure the idea was to get past you, climb the valley wall an' head south-west over The Plateau. I heard the Boss sayin' somethin' about Skull Canyon. It'd be sense for 'em to come out there' – that way they'd be clear of you fellas."

"I'm goin' after 'em," Jason Shepherd snapped. "I'm gonna get that goddam Cash in my sights if it's the last durned thing I do."

"I'm with you," Royle said. "I gotta personal score to settle with Boss Quinn after him gettin' my well blowed up. I reckon they can't be that far ahead of us, they couldn't travel fast in the rain and darkness."

Jason Shepherd nodded and turned to the trembling Circle-Star man. "Okay, Curtis, go an' tell your pals to come out, minus their shootin' irons. Any sassy ideas an' my boys will be only too pleased to ventilate 'em."

"I ain't gonna go through that water again," declared Curtis with conviction. "There's a blamed current which comes round the side of the house that could carry a man off. I'll signal 'em."

He turned and waved his soaking banner of truce above his head. Soon other figures appeared through the door and began wading towards the victors. All, except those who were helping a couple of wounded comrades, held their hands level with their shoulders. It was clear the fight had gone out of them. Soon they were on their way in a miserable procession towards Silver Bend. The Cattlemen's Protection Association astride their shivering mounts, rode behind them but did not bother to keep their guns un-holstered. Some of them even offered the prisoners dry tobacco.

By mid-morning the rain stopped and the ground began to steam strangely, while the distant roar of water foaming over Boss Quinn's dam gradually faded.

On the top of The Plateau, Royle and Jason Shepherd walked in silence. Like all men born to the saddle, they had an inbred dislike of walking and each mentally cursed the fact that they could not take horses up the steep valley wall. Their only consolation was that the two men ahead of them were in the same plight.

Royle had a grudging admiration for Boss Quinn. Climbing up to the top of The Plateau had been a hard enough job in the daylight, and it must have been ten times worse in the rain drenched darkness.

About noon Jason broke the silence. "Reckon in another hour we should reach Skull Canyon," he said.

Royle grunted. He still had vivid and now bitter recollections of the place with its weird rock formations. It was strange he was now returning to it to hunt down the father of the girl who had first showed it to him.

But Royle did not dwell long on the complexities of the feud. Something had happened to him during the water war, yet it was not the bullets which had come his way that had bred a hatred for the Circle-Star boss, it was the destruction of his handiwork. He realised with surprise he had only felt so outraged once before in his life, when he found rustlers driving off cattle from his father's small ranch in New Mexico.

At this moment, however, he spared little thought for the past as he did for the future. His love for Ella was as dead as his love for Linda had become long, long ago when a letter was handed to him by a warder, telling him she had married Ethan. All that mattered now was that he catch up with Boss Quinn and Sam Cash. There was an inevitability about this final meeting and he wanted to get it over.

A little while later there came the distant sound of gunfire.

"That's sure from Skull Canyon way," said Jason.

"Mebbe it's them," Royle said. "They're sure usin' some lead. Maybe they've met some of our boys."

The shooting continued spasmodically until the two men finally reached the lip of the canyon. Here they looked down into the great cleft, but as it curved continuously it was impossible to see far along it.

"I figure they're round that far bend there," said Jason, lowering himself over the edge.

"Yeah, isn't that where the skull rock is?"

The settler nodded. Next minute both men were climbing down the side. Wind and rain had carved the canyon into strange shapes. Here and there on the skyline were formations of soft white rock like the turrets and battlements of castles, in other parts the cliffs looked like cascades that had suddenly become petrified. Luckily the rock face down which they were climbing was full of crevasses and cracks, providing plenty of handholds and narrow ledges.

The gunfire continued, its echo bouncing from rock face to rock face until the whole canyon was alive with its thunder.

The two men reached the bottom, and, with their guns drawn, were now leaping from boulder to boulder, sliding down treacherous slopes of pebbles and climbing over grotesque masses of delicately-hued rock.

Following the rain, a stream found its way down the centre of the canyon, gushing down a series of giant steps like quicksilver. Royle, who was ahead of Jason, splashed through a swirling pool and, skirting a great shoulder of pink granite, found himself looking down another vista of the canyon.

He immediately held up his left hand to warn Jason Shepherd, who came panting behind him, to be quiet.

"Gawd a'mighty," he wheezed. "A war party!"

"Looks like one of Howlin' Wolf's bands."

The distant Indians, about a dozen of them, lay in a

semi-circle with their backs to Royle and Shepherd. Crouched behind rocks, they were firing at the opening of a shallow cave which appeared like a grinning mouth in a bizarre skull-shaped formation which gave the canyon its name. Gunsmoke drifted from it, and at intervals spurts of flame cut its darkness. The Indians were returning the fire, five had guns, the others were armed with bows and lances. All the time they were endeavouring to squirm closer and closer to the dark skull mouth.

As they watched, a brave rose with his rifle but before he could fire a shot toppled him backwards among a patch of boulders. His shrill scream lived for several seconds after him as the echoes of the canyon mocked it.

One of his comrades bent over him to take the rifle.

"They got 'em holed up all right," said Shepherd. "Jest a matter of time before they send 'em to the Happy Huntin' Ground."

"We can't let them redskins take their scalps," said Royle, moving forward.

Without a word his companion followed him. Like two shadows they slipped from rock to rock until they were within effective range for their Colts. The braves were too interested in the defenders of the skull to notice the two palefaces behind them.

Carefully Royle selected a shelf of rock and stretched himself along it. He unbuckled his cartridge belt and laid it in front of him so he could replenish the chambers of the Frontier quickly.

Jason Shepherd took up position behind a boulder about fifty feet away so that the braves would not have targets close together. Royle glanced over to Jason and raised his hand in a mock salute. Jason returned it, and both men squinted down their gun barrels. Royle held his sights on the back of an Indian who was crawling forward with the rifle he had taken from the dead warrior.

Gently he squeezed the trigger so as not to jerk the

Frontier. The hammer fell and the Indian jerked like a fish suddenly flipped from the water. A second later Jason's gun crashed.

The Indians turned, yelling to each other. The two Colts crashed again and again, and one of the braves threw his hands up to his face. Caught in a cross fire, the Indians began to retreat down the canyon, firing as they went. An arrow hit the rock wall above Royle and snapped in two. A bullet left a silvery trail on the limestone beside him.

He swore when his sixth bullet had gone. He hastily swung out the cylinder and began to empty the chambers of the used cartridge cases. As he did this the firing continued from the cave mouth, and another Indian toppled, falling into the fast moving stream.

Within a couple of minutes of Royle's first shot the battle was over the remaining Indians were in flight down the canyon.

"Guess they must have thought we was half a troop of soldiers," laughed Jason. " Let's go see what's happened to them coyotes in the cave."

He ran forward, not noticing a figure that rose from the shadow of the rocks. Across his face was a single bar of white which gave it a terrifying appearance. Now he raised a long-barrelled gun and fired at the hated white man.

The ball caught Jason just above the right elbow, turning his sleeve to crimson. Royle cursed his empty gun and fumbled to reload. The Indian had thrown down the gun and, drawing a knife, leapt at Jason Shepherd who was trying to retrieve his gun with his left hand. The burly settler was borne down by the savage onslaught of the oiled brave. The knife rose in the air, then the brave coughed and became horribly limp, like a full-size rag doll. Slowly Jason got to his feet and looked up. At the mouth of the skull stood Sam Cash, a ribbon of smoke drifting from the muzzle of his Navy Colt.

For a long, long moment the two men looked at each other, then Jason said shakily: "Thanks Sam, I thought I was a goner."

Royle and Shepherd clambered up to the cave mouth, where they saw Boss Quinn lying on his side. From his back protruded a brightly feathered arrow. A scarlet thread ran from his mouth, staining his beard.

Royle bent close to him.

"How is it, old-timer?" he asked.

Boss Quinn gave a small twisted smile. " It ain't all that bad," he whispered. "It's like when I was hid in a water butt one time – I was terrified until suddenly I looked up an' there was my Dad – an' I suddenly felt everythin' was okay an' I didn't need to worry no more – that's what it's like now – sorta peaceful."

"What can I do for you?" asked Royle.

"Ain't much you can do for me, son," Quinn gasped, sweat suddenly beading his forehead. "I'm – runnin' outa time. Ain't it strange – life repeats itself – it were an Indian arrow that killed my Dad – guess it must run in the family – Listen, son, there's something you can do – go an' find Ella – the Circle-Star will be hers now – she really loves you, son, that's why she's acted like she has – an' I guess she'll need you now – guess she's headed to Tucson to her mother – go after her, bring her back – times are a-changing an' the ranch'll need you both –"

"I'll do that, old man," said Royle quietly.

Boss Quinn began to cough, a spasm of pain twisted his features.

"It's that goddam arrow," he muttered. "Pull it out, will ya –?"

Royle shook his head slightly.

"I can't go with that goddam thing stickin' outa me," murmured Boss Quinn. "Ain't dignified –"

Royle seized the shaft, closed his eyes and pulled hard.

Boss Quinn gave a slight moan, and then smiled up at the man bending over him.

"It's like I said, kinda peaceful – funny thing – why did we go on – fightin' – when the – drought broke –?"

* * *

Royle and Sam Cash stood at the entrance to Skull Canyon, ahead of them the plain stretched to the horizon. The sky was a mild blue, the rain clouds having been replaced by high cirrocumulus which looked like a celestial flock of sheep. The harshness of the drought had gone. Somewhere a bird was singing.

Jason Shepherd, his arm in a sling, had left them, riding back to Silver Bend on one of the dead Indians' ponies.

"You aimin' to do anythin' particular?" inquired Sam Cash.

"I aim to get a cayuse an' head for Arizona."

"That figures. I was thinkin' of headin' that way myself. I reckon – seein' the war's over – we might hit the trail together –"

"Sure thing, Sam," said Royle. "It's a long way an' it'll give me a chance to get them silver spurs back."

Sam Cash grinned, and the two men began walking south. Soon they were lost in the vastness of the silent plain.